Generation Gap

Alex McGilvery

celticfrog Publishing

Generation Gap

Copyright © 2017 by Alex McGilvery

For information contact :

http://alexmcgilvery.com

Cover design by Victorine Lieske

Second Edition: July 2018

Sax and Whisky

Joe sipped his whisky. It burned on his tongue like the sound of the blues player rolling across his ears. He gave fervent thanks his ability to appreciate the music hadn't diminished over the years.

He sat at a small table to the side of the club close enough to see the saxophonist's fingers blur, but far enough away to allow the harmonies to absorb texture from the conversations surrounding him. He let himself blend into the background, just one more old man in a room of old people. Occasionally someone would sit at his table, but after a glance from Joe, would move on to another table or back to the bar as if something about Joe made them uncomfortable. His job and his age had that effect on people.

The waitress came with the next round and he nodded at her. She smiled at him, giving him another chance to admire her. Whether her teeth were real or not, her dentist was a genius.

Joe looked around at the club. The octogenarian crowd, still full of themselves after making it to retirement, filled the club. The only Youngers in the room were the musicians and the bartender with the discreet caduceus on his shirt and the medical kit hidden behind the bar.

The set concluded, and the player came over to Joe's table. Joe waved at him to sit. With a nervous glance the younger man took a seat. The musician attracted some attention. A few raised eyebrows at Joe, others just shifted their chairs to turn their backs. The other musicians were backstage, probably in a stark concrete room. No Youngers would dare come to the tables unless someone like Joe invited them. New retirees didn't like rubbing shoulders with youth.

"That's sweet playing, son," Joe said.

"Thank you, sir. I love the music." He wiped a faint sheen of sweat from his face.

Poor kid was hardly forty.

"My name is David." He twitched nervously as if trying to find a spot which made him invisible.

Joe waved the waitress over.

"Some water for my friend. Music is thirsty work." She brought the water, but set it in front of Joe, refusing to acknowledge the younger man. Joe sighed and pushed the glass across the table.

The musician lifted the glass and drank it at one go. He blushed and put the empty glass back on the table in front of him.

"I can't tell you how much it means to me that you came, sir."

"It's my job, David. But your playing has made it a pleasure. Tell me again about what made you call my office."

"I love playing, I love the music. But I have a problem..."

Joe waited, sipping at his drink. It had tasted better with the music. Conversations provided white noise in the background.

Finally, the young musician looked up, smooth face carefully blank.

"My contract is for music, and just music. I don't mind giving music lessons to the club's owner, but she wants more than music. It's flattering, I guess, but it's creepy. Look at me. I'm only forty. I still have children at home. What does she want with someone like me? Not like there aren't all kinds who'd love to give her what she wants. I just want to play my sax and go home."

Joe sighed and looked at the sax player.

"Do you want a different contract?"

"No way." He flushed. "I mean, this is a great job. I get to play music, and mostly whatever I like. It's just...." His blush deepened. "...if she would just leave me alone."

"All right, son, I'll have a word with her." The musician sat back in relief, and Joe sipped at his drink again. He levered himself up with his cane and walked toward the office.

The door was closed, so he rapped on it with the head of his cane. He heard a scuffling behind the door and a moment later it opened. She wasn't as attractive as the waitress, but she didn't need to be. He saw too many like her. Only a decade past retirement herself, she reminded her customers of their old existence along with the perks of their new lives. Like a lot of people her age - figuring now she'd made it, she could take whatever she wanted. Joe walked into the office without saying anything and looked around. Well set up, if a little soft for his taste. He noted the couch against one wall and frowned. The cushions were still returning to their shape. The door beside the couch hadn't quite closed.

"May I help you?" Her voice was a carefully contrived contralto.

"You can keep your hands off the saxophone player," Joe said.

"What are you? A prude? You don't like the idea I still have needs?"

"I don't care about your needs. Just keep your hands off people who aren't willing."

"He signed a contract!" she screeched, forgetting her contralto. "I can break him just as easily as I made him."

"He signed a contract to provide music for your club. There is no clause forcing him to provide sexual favors to the owner."

"So what? Everyone knows it's part of the deal. I give him a job, he gives me what I want."

Joe leaned forward on his cane. "You keep your hands off the staff, and I will walk out of here and never bother you again. Bother that young man one more time, and I will take this club away from you."

"How dare you talk to me like this!" Her voice rose another octave. "I am retired now. I deserve everything I can get. Do you know what I had to put up with? Do you? No. But you stand here and preach at me about what I can and can't do to my staff. I *own* them."

"I think maybe it's time you went into the Home," Joe said quietly. "It is clear you aren't managing retirement well."

"NO!" she screamed and lunged at him. Joe lifted his cane and stopped her with it. She tried to bat it to one side to get to him, and he pushed a button on the handle. Twenty-thousand volts coursed through her and she dropped twitching to the floor. The not-quite-closed door burst open and the bartender ran in. He had his kit out, and was taking her pulse before his knees hit the floor.

"You may have killed her."

"I knew you were there," Joe said. "I figured you'd save her."

"And if I don't?"

"Then she won't have to spend the rest of her life in the Home, will she?"

The bartender stared at Joe.

"The law is the law, even for retirees. You may want to remember that if you live so long." Joe pointed at the woman on the floor. "Your boss forgot no one is above the law, so one way or the other, her happy retirement is over."

She coughed and her eyes opened.

"Who are you?" she asked.

"I'm a Methuselah," Joe answered, "my job is reminding retirees they may have risen above the need to work, but no one is above the law.'

"I thought you were a myth." Her eyes closed,

but tears out leaked anyway.

"Some days, I wish we were." Joe stepped aside to allow the transport crew in. They strapped the terrified woman onto the gurney and wheeled her out.

The music started up again in the club. Joe paused for a second then went back to his table to listen. He didn't get out very often any more. The music and the whisky mixed in his soul and washed it clean. For a while he let himself forget about the world and his place in it.

At the Reserve

Trey sat in class hating the new teacher. The grey cinderblock room in the U.S. Youth Reserve 27 had just enough windows to save on the cost of lighting. The desks were carefully placed to make sure the students had no distracting views to keep them from learning the lessons the school was determined to teach them. After more than a decade in the Reserve, grey cinderblocks were etched on his soul.

Today the lesson was history—even more tedious than English. Trey slumped farther down into his chair and considered whether he could get away with a quick nap.

"Trey, sit up and pay attention. This will be on the test." Mr. Destir hadn't even turned around. The other boys snickered, and the teacher turned and glared at them. He made no secret of his loathing for this class.

Trey'd heard him complaining to the other teachers the students only had to suffer through the material once. He was stuck with it for the rest of his career, and this was his first year.

Mr. Destir massaged his gut.

"George, please explain the Final Amendment."

George stood up and took a deep breath. Trey made a rude noise just before George started speaking. The whole class laughed and George turned beet red. Mr. Destir ground his teeth and looked at Trey.

"Perhaps, Mr. Gauche, you can do more than provide cheap amusement and explain the Final Amendment."

Trey just stared into space and considered his options. He could crank Mr. Destir up a few more notches before he was sent to the office. Yawning as widely as he could, he looked innocently at the teacher.

"Sorry, I didn't hear you, sir."

Mr. Destir glared at Trey. He clenched his teeth and repeated the question.

"Uh, the Final Amendment... that would be the law that took all rights from everyone who isn't an old fart. It would also be the reason why you are here trying to teach stuff no one in their right mind wants to learn."

The crack of the yardstick shattering across his desk caused Trey to startle and fall off his chair. As Trey lay on the floor, Mr. Destir gripped the broken ruler like a knife. For an instant, Trey prepared himself for the pain if his teacher stabbed him. Instead the bell rang and Mr. Destir shook himself.

"You will have a thousand-word paper on the subject of the Final Amendment on my desk tomorrow morning." He walked back to the desk, sat down and watched the class file out. When Trey passed in front of Mr. Destir, the teacher's hand stroked the broken ruler. Trey shuddered and almost ran from the room. But when the Principal brushed past him, he crouched against the wall and fiddled with his shoelace while he listened.

"Well, Harry, I was beginning to wonder if you had it in you," the Principal said.

"Pardon me?"

"About time you realized you're teaching a room full of hooligans who have no interest in learning. You have to force them to respond so your success rating will stay up." The Principal was an imposing man whose red face made Trey doubt he would survive to retire. "It isn't about what the reprobates want. It's what we want. We want to be paid. We want to retire someday. Who cares about the snot-noses? Half of them will end up in the transplant bank before they're twenty. Take care of yourself, keep them in line, and maybe one of them will learn something by accident."

"I did consider bringing a knife to school and disemboweling the little bastard in front of the class. It would likely aid discipline, though I imagine the administration would not be pleased."

"Ha! It's good to see you still have a sense of humor." With a slap on Mr. Destir's shoulder the Principal left the room. "Keep it up, Harry. I'll be watching you."

"I wasn't joking," Trey heard as he hurried on to the next torture session disguised as education.

The following morning, the class filed in and sat down. They waited to see what would happen next. Mr. Destir had a new ruler. It sat on his desk glinting metallically in the harsh light.

As he sat down Trey heard a whisper from behind him.

"Way to go, Lefty. There'll be no living with him now."

Trey shrugged and focused his attention on the front of the room. *Score one for the old farts, but I'm not done yet.* Mr. Destir taught with new confidence. Silently Trey agreed with the whisperer. Destir had found a way to deal with his disruptive class. The ruler lay on the desk, untouched, unmentioned, but at the front of everyone's mind.

Trey's job was to distract the teachers and make life easier on the other boys in his class. In exchange Hank and his other roommates protected Trey from the other students. During his early years at the Reserve, Trey had used his sharp wit and acid tongue on any target presenting itself. Hank stepped in after Trey had been left bruised and unconscious in the showers for the third time.

"You want to die, you're going the right way." Even then Hank had towered over Trey. "What's your name, kid?" Hank asked as he mopped blood from Trey's face.

"Trey Gauche."

"What kind of name is that?"

"It means Three Left."

"Left of what?"

"No, like left, right."

"Right, Lefty, you'll bunk with me and my mates from now on. Turn those smarts on the teachers and distract them from the rest of us, and I'll keep you in one piece."

The nickname sealed the deal.

Mr. Destir would need more work. After yesterday's eavesdropping, Trey might want to keep an eye out for weapons sharper than the ruler. Trey kept his head down for the rest of the class. He dropped his paper on the desk on his way out. It should give Mr. Destir more heartburn.

Next day, Mr. Destir asked Trey to wait after class.

"I'm surprised at the essay you handed in, Trey. It's a very cogent treatment of the Final Amendment. I am not sure about some of the conclusions you reach. I don't think you can draw a direct line from the medical advances in gerontology to the disenfranchisement of youth."

"Of course there is a direct relationship. Old people started living not just longer, but better. Their bodies didn't betray them to a long, slow decline anymore, and they wanted to spend the money they had saved. The old held on to their money instead of passing it to the next generation. They wanted to keep the world the way they knew it, so gradually laws were enacted forcing younger generations to the fringe of society. Soon only the old were able to hold office, while the young desperately tried to scrabble enough money together to retire."

"But the retirees were just living out what they had earned through their lives."

"Naw, the real power still lay with the people with money. The rich folks could afford the drugs and the treatments. They have the money to live comfortably for decades past retirement. Poor people can't afford health care, so they never make it to retirement. It isn't a big stretch to move the voting age to the retirement age, and to mandate a minimum bank account to be allowed to retire. You know what happens to the poor people if they live too long. Off to the Home—warehoused until they die."

"Trey, what are you doing in this class?" Mr. Destir leaned back and looked at Trey with something dangerously close to approval.

"I'm an illegal—a third. My father wanted to have someone who was a close match in case he needed some spare parts. He had enough pull to have me carried to term, but not enough to hide me for long. So I get dumped in the Youth Reserve. I'll be safe and well fed. If I'm lucky dear old dad will never require any kind of transplant. So I'll just get sent to some dead end job until I die. If he does need my organs, it will only be a matter of time before I suffer an unfortunate accident. His crime wasn't so much having too many children, as being crass enough to get caught." Trey paced up and down in front of the desk, too caught up in his argument to care about the consequences of his opinions. "Do you know what chance I have of surviving to retirement? None, zero, zip. The retirees want it that way. I'm spare parts. My brains are only an unfortunate side effect."

Mr. Destir shook his head and sat behind his

desk. "I admit our system has its flaws, but it's not as bad as you say. You have the right facts, but you chose the worst interpretation. What am I going to do with you?"

"Nothing, there is nothing to be done with me. I barely exist. I'll get through this year, get a crappy contract the next, and if I'm lucky will die messily enough he won't be able to use any of my parts to keep himself-" Trey stopped abruptly and unclenched his fists. *How could I fall for his dirty trick. He's not interested in what I think, just in shutting me up.*

"I think I am going to have to give you detention, young man. You will have to sit here every day after school, and we will talk."

"I haven't done anything to deserve detention."

"Not yet," Mr. Destir dismissed him.

GOING OVER THE WALL

"Hey Lefty." Hank plunked his food down beside Trey's. "How're you hanging? You been doing detention with Destir for weeks."

"I guess the ruler thing was a bit overdone," Trey admitted.

"You guess? I never seen someone that mad. What does he make you do?" Hank poured bright orange drink into his glass.

"He just talks with me. I think he's made me his special project."

"Well at least he's leaving *me* alone. *Talk*." Hank shuddered. "It's unnatural."

Hank settled down to shovel his huge plate of food into his mouth. He was the biggest bully in a school full of bullies for good reason. Trey picked at his food. Even if he wanted, he couldn't eat like Hank who was at least twice Trey's size. Good thing Hank was on his side.

Trey didn't want to chat with Harry Destir, but every day his mouth would start spouting off everything his brain concocted and Harry'd listen. Then they'd argue. Words were the pieces in their intellectual chess game. Trey hated him and needed him at the same time.

As the year progressed, Trey's behavior in class got worse. Harry bashed Trey's desk with the steel ruler until it looked like a relic from the war movies they watched for recreation. He laughed about it after school. In return Trey ramped up his torment of his other teachers, punishing them for not being as quick as he was.

Trey hated himself for enjoying his time with Harry. The sad truth was he'd become addicted to someone taking him seriously. Harry actually challenged him to think harder instead of forcing him to hide his intellect under a veneer of delinquency.

His classmates were beginning to suspect the relationship was outside the boundaries, but they thought in terms of sex. They looked at him with pity, and otherwise ignored him as "tainted". Trey tried not to care. His classmates knew no more about girls than they did about history, though they cared more about girls. All the inmates and staff on the Youth Reserve were male. Females were housed a hundred miles to the south. Most plans for escaping their fate included heading down to the girls' reserve. Trey didn't expect to live long enough to get involved with girls.

He knew what was going to happen. It was just a matter of time, but he couldn't bring himself to do anything more than make vaguely paranoid comments to Harry. The term was almost over when the Principal walked in on the 'detention'.

Trey couldn't decide whether Harry or the Principal was the more surprised. Harry, because he couldn't imagine he was being watched or the principal, because he was expecting something more along the line of what Trey's classmates suspected. From the dumbfounded look on his face, he would have been much happier to find one of them with his pants down. Instead he had interrupted Trey in the middle of yet another denunciation of the geritocracy which had quietly, and without resistance, overthrown the democratic processes of their country.

"Ahem" The Principal's face was even redder than its usual florid tones. "I don't think this is a helpful conversation."

"What about free speech?" Trey asked, already knowing the answer.

"Free speech is limited to those with the wisdom to exercise it."

"Just like everything else in this world. Only the old have the wisdom to use the power, which only they are allowed to have. The young are nothing but slaves or worse."

Harry made shushing motions at Trey, but they were already as good as dead. *Might as well go down in flames.*

"We live in a great country, boy. We're at peace, no one goes hungry, no one is without shelter."

"We're behind the rest of the world and falling further behind every year. There are no new ideas, because all the control is in the hands of old farts who would die before taking any kind of risk."

"You're very bitter for someone who is getting the best education in the world, along with room and board and all without any cost to you." The Principal crowded Trey, towering over him and engulfing him in a cloud of pungent odor.

"You *are* joking, aren't you? Even someone like you should be able to see we are being primed for short, brutal lives. There are huge gaps in what is being 'taught' and what we need to know." Trey refused to step back, but glared up into the bulging eyes of the principal.

"Careful, boy. You're treading on dangerous ground."

"I've been on dangerous ground since the day the Methuselahs caught my dad with an extra kid carrying his genes. You know as well as I do, they stuck me here just in case they need my high quality organs. Some of the Geris don't like accepting transplants from the peons."

"That is quite enough, young man. You will take yourself off to your room and I will deal with you later." The now purple-faced principal turned to the thunderstruck teacher.

"No." Trey fought the urge to hang his head and run to his room. "You know I'm right. I'll bet you're just waiting until you retire so you can get your share of the organs they process through this place."

The Principal turned and stared at Trey while Harry covered his eyes with his hand.

"Are you disobeying me?" He grabbed the ruler

off the desk. "You ungrateful punk, do you know how many years I have been trying to help people like you?" He swung the ruler at Trey and caught him across the face. Trey backed up and tripped over a desk. The principal lumbered up and kicked at the young man. Mr. Destir grabbed the Principal from behind and tried to pull him back. Instead the Principal, his face still purple, turned and swung at his subordinate.

"You are fired. FIRED. I will make sure you never..." The ruler fell with a clatter as the Principal clutched his chest. His florid face suddenly turned white and he collapsed to the floor.

"Help me.... medication...in office....go. Password is December, I was supposed to retire..." His head fell back.

Trey and Mr. Destir stared at the form of the man who, seconds before had held the power to destroy their lives. Killing the Principal might even be worse than sedition.

"Oh dear." Harry sat abruptly in his chair. "Now what do we do?"

"We can call the Administration and someone will come and clean up the mess." Trey still lay on the floor, not sure his legs would hold him yet. "But I think you'll find we're part of the mess. The Geris don't like this kind of business. I'm leaving. Now, before they get here to find out I was in the middle of this. I'm fairly sure my value as a bargaining chip with my old man won't keep them from pinning this on me and parting me out." Trey pushed himself to his feet and took a careful breath. "I don't think he broke anything." He limped toward the door. "It's been real."

"Wait." Harry held up his hand then let it drop. "If you wait until dark you'll have a better chance." Harry shrugged. "I'll close the door and keep his death quiet as long as I can. Good luck, lad."

Trey stared at Harry then shrugged, too and went out the door.

He didn't meet anyone on the way to the room he shared with Hank and two other boys. All three were relaxing on Hank's bed playing cards. They glanced up then stared at Trey's face. He was sure there was a huge red mark where the ruler had hit. A glance in their mirror showed he'd underestimated the damage. A thin red line oozed blood, while the skin around it had turned a sullen purple. He smiled at himself. Terrific, maybe it would scar and he could spend his life explaining how he'd been marked by a teacher's ruler.

"What happened to you?"

"I shouldn't have used my teeth," Trey said with an inward apology to Mr. Destir. In the awestruck silence greeting his remark he went over to the single drawer he was allowed and turned all his clothes onto the bed. It was a matter of seconds to sort through the pile and roll up the couple of spare shirts and pants. He put them into his pillowcase.

"What are you doing?" Hank loomed over him.

"I'm going over the wall," Trey looked around for anything else that might be useful. Hank went to his drawer and reached all the way to the back. He pulled out a crudely shaped knife with a rope handle.

"Here." Hank pushed the knife into Trey's hand. "I can always make another one." He turned back to the cards and the others followed his example. Trey put the blade into the makeshift bag and left the room without another word.

On the other side of the exercise yard's dull grey walls was the outside - no fence, no guards. This was supposed to be a Reserve, not a prison, but the yard with the gate to the outside was still out of bounds. All the boys knew stories of wall jumpers being caught, the news made a big show of capturing runaways, but no one who left the reserve returned. The popular theory said runners were cut up for organs.

Trey dropped his bag in a corner and picked up a basketball. He shot hoops until dark. Some other boys came into the yard, but after a glance at his face they let him be. The dinner bell rang before darkness fell, so Trey left the bag in the corner and went to eat. He struggled to choke down the tasteless food. The cut throbbed and chewing was painful.

The room monitors seemed to have developed selective blindness. Not one of the older students came to ask about his face. Whispers floated around him, but he did his best to ignore them. He didn't know the reasons but he was glad to be left alone. As Trey placed the dishes on the rack someone bumped him and whispered, "Good luck." Trey walked out of the room for the last time.

Grief or anger he'd expected, but not the

depth of relief he experienced at the possibility of escape from the harsh, soul-crushing expectation of a wasted life.

He went straight to the yard and found his bag. He stared at the eight-foot wall and wondered how he was going to get over.

"Need a boost?" Hank stood in the shadows. "When you get over, go to your left 'til you find the ravine. Follow the water to the road then head north. Don't go south, you'd just be asking for trouble. Follow the signs, and you'll be OK. The Underground will find you." He made a stirrup with his hands, and without effort lifted Trey to the top of the wall. "Good luck. You ain't the first to go over the wall, won't be the last." He melted back into the shadows.

Trey dropped his bag then awkwardly lowered himself to the other side. Bag over his shoulder, he headed toward his left.

The directions had sounded clear and easy on the other side of the wall. He hadn't been outside the compound since the Methuselahs had sent him there as a scared little kid. However much he detested the Reserve, it had been home for most of his life.

He slipped on the rocks as he stumbled through the dark, wet ravine. Very quickly he learned, apart from the discomfort, it was easier to walk down the middle of the creek running through the gulley. He focused so much on putting one foot in front of the other he almost missed the road.

As he climbed up the steep slope to the pavement, Trey reviewed Hank's instructions. *Walk north*, but Trey had no idea what was north or south.

He sat on the side of the road and rested. The sky lightened in front of him. The moon rose in the same direction as the sun. So facing east, north was to his left. Trey forced himself to his feet. He stayed to the side of the road, but saw no signs of life.

By the time the sun began to lift above the horizon, Trey's clothes were dry and he staggered with exhaustion. A scraggly stand trees off to one side of the road promised minimal shelter. He found a pile of leaves under a tree and curled up. There was something he was forgetting, but he fell asleep before he could figure it out.

The afternoon found him waking stiff and itchy from the leaves. He pulled over his sack to see what a sorry collection he had to survive. Extra clothes, Hank's knife, a pack of matches he wasn't sure would work. He put fresh clothes on. The knife went in his boot. When he put the matches in his pocket his hand brushed something. A napkin. He remembered the bump and the whispered *good luck.* Trey pulled it out and read the words scrawled across it.

> Follow the signs. Each sign will be a circle with a number in it. The number is the approximate number of hours to reach the next sign. A line will point out from the circle. The top of the circle will be North. Travel in the direction the line points. The last thing will be a symbol of something. A tree, a bridge, a house; the sign will be marked on a tree, bridge or house. It will be marked on the same side of the object,

as the symbol is to the circle.
If you don't understand, you don't deserve to find the end.

Under the instructions was a circle with the line pointing straight up. On the left was a picture of a tree with three trunks. Trey tore the napkin to pieces and hid them under the leaves. Being caught with the napkin would be worse than getting lost, and the instructions were clear enough.

R E D

It took a little longer than the five hours the napkin had estimated to find the trees. The light was gone by then, so Trey sat with his back to their trunks and tried to sleep. He nodded off a few times, but cold and hunger kept him awake for the most part. He'd have to scrounge something to eat tomorrow.

The napkin suggested an organized group who weren't friendly to the Geris - a group combining daring, craftiness and determination, to have people placed in the Youth Reserves. Trey looked forward to meeting them.

When the sun rose he found the second sign carved into a tree. He didn't know much about trees, but the carving didn't look fresh.

Trey's stomach rumbled as he walked east along a dirt road. No choice but to ignore the pangs and keep moving. All through the day and into the night his stomach gnawed while he avoided people, and thus sources of food. Growing up in the Reserve meant he knew nothing about what was edible around him.

Days stretched out as he walked and tried to remember if he knew how many days a human could go without food. He drank water from streams in the woods avoiding dangers in human form.

While he skirted around a village, a black shape bounded toward him -a dog, its eyes glowing red lasers. A fence separated them, but the animal headed toward a low gate.

Trey stumbled into a run away from the animal. He had maybe a hundred yards lead. Even at his best he couldn't out run the beast, and hunger made him far from his best. Outsmarting it would have to do.

The sound of rushing water drew him. Some of the tattered mystery books left at the Reserve talked about water confusing tracking dogs. Trey crested a hill and saw a large pond with a wheel beside a big building churning water at the far end.

Growling sounded an incalculable distance behind him. Gravity pulled him into longer strides. Trey windmilled his arms to stay on his feet. Without slowing, he plunged into the water.

The pond was deeper than he expected, good for escaping the dog, not so good for a kid who had never swum before. Weeds grew in profusion, so Trey pulled himself along, grasping the wiry stems. He hadn't been under long when his lungs burned and he had to fight the impulse to breathe. His hand hit mud instead of weeds so he clawed his way to the surface and gasped as quietly as he could.

The dog walked around the pond, its nose sniffing at the grass. Trey's heart pounded as the dog's whines passed over his head. Maybe its electronics meant it didn't like water. Trey let himself sink deeper and spread mud on his face. After one circuit of the pond the dog's head lifted and it loped away. The same thing keeping it out of the water let it communicate with the Geri's. Trey had better get moving.

Trey couldn't climb out from his hiding place. He slowly circled the pond until he'd almost reached the wheel. A ladder led up the side of the building so he washed as much of the mud away as he could, then climbed. Trey kept the hill between him and the village until he needed to find the next circle. Walking warmed him and dried his clothes, but did little about the reek of swamp emanating from them.

His path zigzagged along old roads and abandoned tracks, but the general direction was east. Then he found a marker saying the next one was on the side of a house.

From under some brush, Trey examined the little house on the edge of a town. Sure enough the circle was there, disguised as a wreath on the door. In the center was the knocker. Nothing else to do but hope he was at the right place. He crawled out of the brush and headed to the house.

Trey knocked. It took him a moment to realize the person who answered was a woman. She waved him in and led him to a back room. Fog swirled through his brain and sapped his energy. He couldn't even worry about whether he should trust her.

"Poor dears, you always look so starved." Her voice was high and melodic as she pushed him into a chair and set a glass of milk in front of him. "That will keep you until the soup heats up."

Trey tried to thank her, but it was just too much work to talk. Instead he sipped at the milk. By the time he was done there was a steaming bowl of chicken noodle soup in front of him. He started on the soup. He had barely finished before he started nodding off. The woman pulled him to his feet and guided him to a back room with a cot. He was asleep before she closed the door.

Strange smells woke Trey. Fresh clothes lay at the foot of the bed. He changed quickly before following the odor out to the kitchen.

The woman smiled at him and slid a plate with golden brown disc-shaped objects on it. She poured some brown syrupy goo on them and nodded encouragingly. Trey took up the knife and fork and tried a bite. The next thing he knew he had eaten four plates of the 'pancakes' as his host called them.

"I am not supposed to try to explain anything to you. I just feed you and warn you to watch for the dogbots." She sighed at his look of puzzlement. "I know, I know, never heard of dogbots. Dogs that have been adapted with new sensors to detect the nanos in the food they feed you. It takes a while for them to disappear. I'm afraid you are in for another hungry time to finish starving the nanos. The people you're looking for gave me something to add to my rations, which doesn't feed them. Don't ask me how it works." She tapped the refrigerator and whisked the plates off to the dishwasher. Sure enough there was another sign on the appliance's white door.

"Thank you." He beamed a smile at her and waved as he left the house.

***

The new sign sent him south, away from town. Now that he'd eaten, he started finding the markers closer to the estimated times in the circle. That day and the next he walked south. Oddly he didn't see any people after leaving the little house. Only once had he seen a vehicle. Feeling silly he'd hidden off the road. The truck had rumbled by, but there was no driver.

The hunger pangs came on then faded, and his pace slowed again.

At the edge of a city Trey followed the signs into a dark deserted neighborhood. A few people strolled in the distance, but paid no attention to him. In the city he got a closer look at a dogbot.

It came around a corner in the alley as he shuffled along. The thing had a metal skullcap and its two lasers glowed red. Instead of sniffing the ground like dogs in books did, it waved its head back and forth. It stared straight at Trey and his hands went clammy. The dog tested the air, the luminous red eyes scanned him, but whatever it was seeking was absent. No longer engaged, it wandered away.

The signs started taking on more complexity, showing miniature maps resembling scratches or writing. Increasingly, the guides were concealed, and Trey spent almost as much time searching for them as he did walking.

Trey might as well have been a ghost, wandering the streets studying boarded up stores and closed factories. Weeds grew through the cracked pavement in places. Dogbots passed in the distance each one seemed to examine and then dismiss him, but they still made him nervous.

He found the last sign under a bridge - a circle with a dot in the middle, nothing else. Trey waited, hunched over, trying to avoid touching the filthy floor. Graffiti covered the concrete making the final sign look like one more tag. From what Trey could surmise, the graffiti artists weren't happy. Even with a bright sunny day a few feet away, the underpass made the air dark and damp. The gloomy setting suited him just fine. His mood was even darker. Trey was hungry, tired, and scared spitless – *"What do I do now?"*

Just as Trey was deciding he should move on, a grinding sound echoed from the road. An access cover lifted out of the mud and clanged on the ground. The most outrageously dressed person Trey had ever seen lifted herself out of the sewer.

"Been waiting long?" She wore a black form-fitting suit with red pieces to make it very clear she was indeed female. "Hey, cat's got your tongue? You never seen a girl before?"

"Not like you." Trey shook his head and tried to get his brain working. He pushed himself erect to look her in the eye.

"Thanks, that's the nicest thing you've said to me all day." She smiled at him, increasing both his confusion and the strange feelings just a little south of his stomach.

"Who are you?"

"Call me Red," she said. "Good enough for a first date. Are you ready to join us?"

"I'm Trey," he said. "You mean there are more of you?"

"Well not like me. I'm one of a kind." She winked. "That might be a good thing. So, are you coming?"

"Coming where?" Trey asked. "Joining who? You aren't making any sense."

"How long since you ate?" Red asked.

"It must be at least a week." Trey groaned.

"Hmmm, maybe the drugs haven't worn off yet." She smiled at him again. "Listen carefully." She spoke slowly and with exaggerated clarity. "I am asking if you want to join the Underground. If you do, you need to come with me."

"I am not stupid, you know," Trey winced at the whine in his voice. He wanted to shout at her, but it would be a bad idea to annoy the only way out of this place.

"Naw, just still a little drugged." She shrugged - a wholly different action from the boys on the reserve. "You will be fine in a day or so, probably."

Trey shook his head again.

"Drugged?" Even to him, he sounded dumb.

"Sure, the Geris drug all you little darlings. Can't have you risking their spare parts or doing any unplanned procreating."

"Procreating?"

"Not on a first date, Trey." She winked again and wiggled in a way that doubled those strange feelings. "All will be explained."

The crunch of tires on the gravel sounded outside the underpass. The Geris had found him.

"Right on time. The old farts are predictable. Are you coming with me, or going with them?"

"With you," Trey answered, moving away from the wall. The girl grabbed the access cover. He climbed down a ladder into the black hole.

With lithe grace she jumped down into the hole and replaced the cover with just a muffled thump.

"We like to know what dogbot feeds they're following. They won't find us."

"Why down here?" Trey whispered as she took his hand.

"Well duh! We're the *Undergound*" Red pulled him into the dark future.

Alex McGilvery

People are Dying

Joe sat at his desk reviewing files. With his rank he could have had any office in the building, but it suited his sense of correctness to work out of the tiny basement office. He had his desk and swivel seat on rollers, a straight-backed chair for a visitor.

A picture on one wall of a beautiful young woman smiling and holding a baby - his wife and son, both long dead hung on the wall. It embarrassed his visitors, so he kept it visible. He wanted to remind the people who came to his office young people and even babies were a part of their world too. A reality all too many retirees forgot, as if the moment they retired and were given their responsibilities, they forgot their previous life.

Joe understood the life of young people was hard and getting harder. What he couldn't grasp was people trying to erase that entire segment of their lives. There was no shame in being young. You had to be young to get old.

Joe signed the last piece of paperwork from the fiasco at the club. The sax player would be under surveillance for a while. The owner had survived the shock, but had been left with permanent tremors in her hands. The nurses at the Home said they had her on a suicide watch. He didn't like using the cane, but not using it was a worse alternative. The Two Cent Council, as Joe thought of his superiors, didn't like messes. Guns were messy, and a danger to bystanders. The cane was quick and affected only one person at a time. Healthy people usually survived the experience.

He'd hardly picked up the file on the murders he was investigating when a double knock on the door signaled Joe's secretary was showing someone into his office. He looked up to watch as she pushed the door open and ushered in the visitor. Maggie always acted as if his rinky-dink little office was a corner penthouse suite. He liked the way she flashed her teeth in a bright smile. They were implants, but the very best. Her silver hair was pulled back in a loose bun and contrasted nicely with the forest green suit tailored to make the best of her other assets.

As the visitor, who had to be at least a centenarian, stalked into the cramped office, Maggie's fingers moved in sign language. Deputy Chancellor George Mulholland, in line for a Council position if he could keep his nose clean long enough.

"I am told you are the man to help me." The visitor boomed as Maggie discreetly closed the door.

"And what am I helping you with?" Joe waved D.C. Mulholland to the other chair.

"There has been a bit of trouble at the Mid-West Youth Reserve. It seems the Principal was involved in an unfortunate relationship with one of the boys. The Principal died suddenly, and the boy is missing. It is presumed he has run away. There is no sign of him, which suggests he may have had help. Runners are usually caught within a couple of days."

"People die all the time. Young people run away quite frequently. Why do you need me on this case?"

"You know who I am?"

"Yes. Does it have a bearing on this situation?"

"Unfortunately it does." The visiting Deputy Chancellor looked around his eyes lighting on the photo of woman and child. "Yours?" At Joe's nod he continued. "Then you might understand. The boy who has run away is named Trey Gauche, my son. Others have assumed I broke the law to ensure a suitable transplant match if needed, but the truth is I wanted to have a child who shared my intellect. My daughters are a delight, but they are not brilliant."

"And Trey is?"

"I suspect he is smarter than I am, but he's never been tested. My wife found out about him and made sure certain people made all the wrong assumptions. Now they think they have Deputy Chancellor in their pockets because they hold my organ reserve."

The last words were spoken with such distaste Joe knew, whatever other truths were being stretched, the Deputy Chancellor did not view his late-comer son as a living organ bank.

"She has everything she ever wanted except my social connections. My... handlers are not ones to give unnecessary attention to a woman who no longer has any power to help them."

Joe thought briefly of the woman at the club, trying desperately to control her life. He pitied both of them.

"So, what do you want from me?"

"I would like you to investigate, and find the boy. Make sure he doesn't fall into the hands of the people who think they own me. I am about to oppose some reforms they are pushing me to support. I don't want them to hurt Trey to get to me."

"You would change your position if they had Trey?" asked Joe.

"No, but they don't know that, and neither does the boy." Mulholland stood up. "Find him and keep him safe.'

"What issue are you opposing?"

"Would it make a difference if I told you?" When Joe shook his head he said, "Then you don't need to know." He let himself out. Maggie slipped into the office and perched on the chair.

"He liked your picture."

"He did at that."

"So, you are heading west?"

"It looks like it, doesn't it?" Joe looked up at the picture and shrugged. "Make sure the new owner of the club treats the sax player right."

"I will do that, Joe. Be careful. I don't trust people who tell that much truth without being asked. There's something this Mulholland is hiding."

"You too? I'd like to meet this kid who scares him so badly."

****

The flight west was mercifully brief. The weather was the comfortable cool of early fall. Fields were full of automated combines doing whatever it was they did to the golden grain. Joe picked up a driver and headed out to the Reserve.

Joe had looked over the local police report on the flight. Harry Destir had called in the authorities after the Principal had died. The investigation found missing segments from the surveillance tapes. The locals had concluded something had been going on between the Principal and the missing student - not an uncommon problem, as staff weren't given the same medications as the students.

He was met by a youngish teacher, who introduced himself as Harry Destir. For someone so young he didn't talk very much, just showed Joe to the Principal's office and left, saying he had a class to teach.

Heavy wood tones dominated the office. A large window looked out at the plains surrounding the compound. When Joe sat in the office chair behind the desk he gave an involuntary sigh. The thing probably cost what the teachers made in a month. There were no other chairs. Not a place where visitors were welcome. Joe leaned forward to use the override password given him by the police to enter the computer system. Sections of the record had been tampered with, just as the report said; a few minutes here, a half hour there.

What the report didn't mention was on the day of the man's death several hours were missing. Joes didn't like changes in patterns. He pulled up Trey's file and immediately saw the resemblance to the Deputy Chancellor in the sharp bones and the careful way he held his mouth. The boy was much slighter and shorter than Mulholland, but had the same deep red hair.

"What secrets are you hiding?" The file was full of reports of Trey's deteriorating behavior. Each teacher complained about his insolence and disruptive activity; that is, each teacher except Mr. Harry Destir. *Interesting.*

Joe stood and went looking for the teacher, his cane tapping on the terrazzo floors. With the help of a passing janitor he found the room. Mr. Destir leaned against the desk listening to an obviously animated discussion. Once he pointed to a young man at the back who shrugged and said something to set the class laughing. The teacher laughed with them then dismissed them. The boys filed past Joe with careful, curious looks. Joe walked into the room and sat at one of the desks at the front of the room.

"Looks like they enjoy your class."

"It is just a matter of putting the material into their own language." Harry sounded defensive.

"Not many teachers can do that, especially with history. At that age I was more interested in sports and girls."

"Well, there are no girls here to distract them, and I give them extra yard time for doing well."

"A radical approach," Joe said. Why did the younger man look guilty?

"I looked at the files in the Principal's office. A

lot of files have been erased. A bit here and there, then a lot all on the same day." Joe looked at the teacher. "Do you have any idea why?"

"Because I erased them."

Joe just looked at him and raised his eyebrow.

"You're going to find out anyway. The police didn't do much of an investigation. I allowed them to draw their own conclusions. Mr. Hubert, the Principal did die exactly as I described, but not for the reasons they gave."

"So, why did he die?"

"He died because he was a mean old bastard. His only thought was surviving until he retired. The young men who are unfortunate enough to be placed here were just so much cannon fodder to him. Learning wasn't important, just test scores.'

"Those sound like reasons to kill him."

"He was attacking Trey. I had to stop him. His blood pressure killed him."

"Why was he attacking Trey?"

"You read Trey's file. He was brilliant and very troubled. He challenged Hubert's authority. He's the main reason I changed my teaching methods."

"I see." Joe leaned back and put his cane on the desk. "And what were you and Trey doing before Principal Hubert found you?"

"We were talking sedition. Trey thought the Final Amendment turned our country from a democracy to a dictatorship. He called it a Geritocracy."

"Did he now? He sounds like a fascinating young man. I would like to meet him."

"Brilliant doesn't do Trey justice. You won't find

him."

Joe levered himself upright and headed for the door.

"What happens now?" Harry asked.

"I expect you'll keep teaching, and if you work hard you'll keep from becoming a mean old bastard."

"But...."

"I am not concerned with the inner workings of this Youth Reserve. I am concerned about the people who are helping young Trey and others like him." Joe's phone buzzed as he talked. "Perhaps you would excuse me."

"Of course. I don't have another class until after lunch. Take your time." Harry left. Joe imagined him heaving a great breath of relief out there in the hall. He was a nice young man in a world with fewer and fewer places for nice people.

"Joe here."

"There's been another killing, Joe. This one is down toward Florida. The M.O. is the same - two extremely sharp knives, almost no blood. Nobody saw anything unusual. The victim was a supervisor just five years from retirement."

"And the other part of the pattern?" Joe heard Maggie's sigh at the other end of the connection.

"He was procuring children. He would approach a poor family and offer to find their children an apprenticeship in his jurisdiction. The children would disappear. The families wouldn't complain because they had "sold" their children. And how could we be letting this happen?"

"There are only so many of us, and a lot more of the really twisted ones. I don't feel sorry for him, but I worry about this person who is dispensing such summary justice. What will happen when they make a mistake?"

"I will have the locals send you the reports. Knowing you are in the loop will make them extra careful."

"Thanks, Maggie. I am going to send you a picture. I want you to do a search through the dogbot network and see if there are any hits. I'll be home soon. Oh, and keep an eye on this Harry Destir. I think he is worth watching. We may be able to give him a nudge or two in the right direction." He closed his phone and stared at the wall.

His response to Maggie was only part of the answer. The other part was the woman at the club. More and more retirees felt entitled to whatever they could take. Younger people got called Youngers and became things instead of people. It worried him because it meant the society he worked for was becoming corrupted.

"A Geritocracy indeed." Suddenly he felt every one of his years weighing upon him, but he couldn't rest yet. He had to find Trey, and learn why this young man terrified his father and made teachers break the law on his behalf.

Meeting the Underground

Trey followed Red through the dank tunnels. They were smooth concrete from what little Trey could see. Red held a light just bright enough to show the path a few feet ahead. His head spun with disconnected thoughts, but every time he tried to sort them out his feet got clumsy and he'd stumble. Red would look back at him and roll her eyes. He didn't know if she was angry or if it was her way of showing pity. Either way he didn't like it. He put his confusion aside and concentrated on following close behind, though that had its own distractions.

Trey was ready to collapse and let Red go on without him when the tunnel joined with a much larger one. An odd looking vehicle waited there - a platform on wheels and a joystick stuck up on the left side with a lamp bolted to the front.

"You will have to hold on," Red said, and Trey jumped. She just smiled as he stared at the bare platform.

"To me, Trey, you will have to hold on to me."

She sighed and pushed him toward the platform. "Lie down facing the front. I will lie beside you. You hold on to me. You touch anything red I will push you off and leave you there." She didn't look like she was joking. Trey lay down carefully, and even more carefully wrapped his left arm around her. "A little tighter, I won't break." She gave him a grin again and kissed him on the cheek.

Trey would have loved to say he would never forget that ride, but the sad truth was he fell asleep before they had gone twenty feet. He must have kept his hands off the red, because the next thing he remembered Red was shaking him awake.

"Just a few steps and you can rest."

He managed to climb the few steps and walked through a door into a room. He fell onto a cot in the corner and let the blankness of sleep take him.

***

Trey was wakened by a firm shake and took a few seconds to review where he was before he studied the person standing in front of him. At least as old as the most senior students at the Reserve, he stood more than a head taller than Trey, and his black clothes fit skintight on a ebony skinned muscular form that would have been the envy of every guy Trey knew.

"Hi, I'm Dan." The stranger held out a huge hand to shake. Trey half expected his hand to be crushed into oblivion, yet Dan's grip was firm, but careful. "I am supposed to get you fed, then show you around."

Trey's stomach made a hopeful twinge and he jumped to his feet. The world went black for a moment and he found himself sitting on the bed again. Not a good start to joining this Underground. *I didn't go through all this to make a fool of myself.*

"Easy, Trey. I don't want to have to carry you."

Trey tried again, slower and managed to stay on his feet. Dan nodded and walked out. Trey followed him down the steps to the tunnel. The platform on wheels was gone. Dan walked ahead with a lamp Trey hadn't noticed, so he followed quickly. They reached a side path and followed it to a dead end.

"Hello, Dan here, with Red's new recruit."

Trey looked around for who Dan spoke to. The concrete split and two massive doors swung open. Dan led him through and the doors shut silently behind them.

On the other side was a chaos of noise and people. They were all Youngers. The oldest he saw was Harry's age. They dressed in everything from Dan's solid black to outfits making Red's look modest. He almost stumbled a few times as he turned his head to get a better look. Each time, Dan's hand would gently grip his arm and hold him until he had his feet under him again. Trey was grateful the big man didn't say anything.

They hadn't walked far before they came to a handful of tables set in the middle of the pavement. Most had people sitting at them, talking, eating, and waving their hands. Dan led him to an empty table.

"Wait here." He walked into a crowd, which

absorbed him, leaving Trey to look around. Lights high up overhead made the space feel outdoors. Trees grew in huge pots. Another level of balconies higher up appeared deserted.

Dan reappeared with a tray of covered dishes. Several others at tables around them had identical trays holding an impressive variety of dishes.

"Eat all you want, but eat slowly. I don't want to clean up any mess." Dan pushed the tray over to Trey.

Trey nodded and started uncovering the array. Remembering the visit at the nameless woman's house he began with soup; then started in on some of the other plates. Just like the pancakes he hardly noticed devouring the rest. He sat back and let out a loud burp.

"Excuse me."

"Ah, don't worry about it." Red slipped into the seat beside him and smiled brightly at Dan.

Dan just sighed.

She nudged him with her elbow. "Dan is a wonderful guy, and all that, but he doesn't talk much. I'm guessing you would like some explanations."

Trey nodded. He liked the warmth of the girl sitting beside him. Somehow it had a different quality than when he sat on crowded benches back at the Reserve. She wore tight blue pants, and a loose translucent shirt. She caught him looking at her.

"Here you are flattering me again." She turned his head away with one finger. "Maybe you will listen better if you look at Dan. Not that he isn't a vision in his own right." Dan rolled his eyes and Red blew a kiss at him. Trey felt a twinge of annoyance that they were so comfortable with each other.

"This," said Red grandly, "is the Underground. Some old rich guy built it as his escape from the ugliness of the world or something ages ago. We found it and turned it into this vision of bliss." Trey heard a few snorts from around him. "Most of us have places outside of the Underground, but there are a few who are full time rebels. We have our own economy and our own rules down here. If you act the youth slave down here, people may laugh at you, but they will forgive you. If you act the rebel against the Geris up there, you will die, or worse." She turned his face toward her. "We are not playing games here. If we are caught, they will kill us. Sometimes you might question how we do things. Save it for down here. Up there," she waved her hand, "we are all business."

"Red's right," Dan said. "some things you can never forget."

"But how do you keep all this hidden from the government? Just the energy signature must be huge."

"Rich old guy, again," Red tapped her head. "Can't have a retreat from the world if everyone can find it. A quarter-mile down there's a molten salt reactor to supply all our energy needs for the next fifty years. He also bribed whoever set up the surveillance in the tunnels so we can control what the cameras show to the computers. All the computers know is algorithms. Show them the right thing and you don't exist. We've hacked into the network on a broader scale, but the more you use that tactic the more likely some bright techie will notice. There are exits to the surface as well as through the tunnels, but they all go through businesses or homes we control."

"But now it's time for Trey to meet our fearless leader." She stood up. "Bring your tray over here." She showed him a rack identical to the one on the Reserve, then led the way into the crowd.

Though Red was shorter than Trey, she walked much faster, winding past booths with piles of clothes or books, electronics, or a mish-mash in heaps. Trey wanted to stop and look, especially at the books, but Red walked past without as much as a glance.

Trey was feeling the need for a rest when she and Dan stopped at a door with no knob. She knocked twice, then three times.

The door swung open to reveal a girl who looked a lot younger than Red. Her hair was bright blue and her eyebrows too. Her icy blue eyes glared at Trey before she smiled at Red. She wore a dress, which flowed from her neck to the floor sleeves touching her fingers.

"Come in. He's expecting you." Her voice was softer than Red's and lower in pitch. Trey felt Red's hand tugging on his so he smiled at the girl and followed Red through the door. Dan left as the door slammed shut behind them. Red led him along a carpeted hallway and around a corner. She stopped and held his hand while she looked at him.

"Listen, Trey," her voice completely unlike her usual bantering tone. "Stay away from Lizzy. She's dangerous. Stare at me all you like. Let your tongue hang out over the girls out there. But when you talk to Lizzy, keep your eyes on her eyes and your hands in plain sight."

"She doesn't look mean," Trey whispered.

"I didn't say mean, I said dangerous, and I meant it. Just be polite and you'll be fine. Never, ever touch her. Not for any reason. If she falls flat on her face in front of you, just wait for her to get up by herself. Not that it will ever happen. I've never seen her be anything but graceful. Come on, now that I have properly scared you." Red said returning to her usual tone. She let go of his hand and walked briskly down the hall and through the wooden door at its end.

They entered a spacious room. What looked like a large window was the biggest screen Trey had ever seen. It showed the outside market with all its color, but none of the noise. Trey caught a glimpse of Dan disappearing into the crowd. He pulled his eyes away from the screen. A man who looked just a little older than Mr. Destir sat at a desk in the corner. He tapped away at a keyboard and muttered into the microphone attached to his earpiece.

For once Red didn't jump right in, but stood and waited silently. Trey followed her example and took some time to examine the room. More computer stations in the corner were vacant. A large, worn rug covered the floor and softened the concrete. Paintings and bookshelves obscured the walls. Several comfortable chairs were set around a large table in one corner. The few rooms Trey had seen so far were variations on concrete grey, but the walls here were painted soft blue.

"So you like my office?" The Chief finished what he was doing and pushed himself out from behind the desk. He sat in a utilitarian wheelchair, legs ending above his knees, and his arms suggested dense muscle. More important was the glint of intelligence in his eyes. Trey walked over and stretched out his hand.

"I'm Trey."

"Pleased to meet you." The man's voice was a light tenor, with a hint of an odd accent. His hand gripped Trey's with as much restrained strength as Dan's. "You might as well call me Chief. Everyone else does. To answer your question about my legs, since everyone is too polite to ask, no I didn't lose them fighting the government, but losing them and...other things is what led me here." He looked at Red. "Someone has activated a search through the dogbots, so could you work your magic and see if you can trace it?" She sat at one of the other stations and began tapping and whispering away. "Please, come sit down." The Chief wheeled himself over the table. Trey flung himself into a chair with a sigh. Red winked at him then went back to work.

"So, what do you think of us so far?"

"I hardly know what to say, sir. If I had known there was a set up like this, I would have run away years ago.'

"One of the reasons we don't let ourselves be better known out there. You aren't the youngest person to arrive here, but we don't like bringing recruits in too early. Whoever is running the country, children are still children, and shouldn't be put in a position of keeping deadly secrets. We're careful about who and when we recruit though we have people in most of the youth reserves. Mostly we create a file for active recruiting later. You're something of a special case, Trey." He slipped a file from a pocket behind his seat, and passed it to Trey. "You know who this is?"

Trey looked at a picture of his father, looking not a day older than the last time he had seen him. The police, accompanied by an old man with cold eyes they addressed as Methuselah Grant, had escorted him from the apartment Trey had shared with his mother. His father had visited occasionally. Trey always knew something wasn't quite right, because other children had fathers who lived with them and were much younger.

The police explained his father had broken the law and Trey would have to go live somewhere else. Trey remembered complaining it wasn't fair. If his father had broken the rules, then *he* should move. That was the only time the cold-eyed Methuselah had spoken. 'Life isn't fair,' he'd said.

It had stayed with Trey since. Life wasn't fair, and Trey didn't expect it to be. Yet there was a part of him deep inside protesting it should be.

"Your disappearance from the Reserve has had no media coverage." The Chief interrupted Trey's memories. "Usually they play up the runaways as dangerous delinquents, complete with tracking dogs and posses of local police. With you, it's like you don't exist. I suspect it has a lot to do with him." The Chief turned the page in the file in front of Trey. The cold-eyed old man stared up at him. "Methuselah Grant. He's one of an elite group who polices the retirees. Unusual for him to be involved in the raid on your home; even more unusual that just weeks after you were taken away to the Reserve your father was made Deputy Chancellor. We think some people are using your existence to control your father. We also think it has heated up in the last few weeks."

"Hey Chief, you'll want to see this." Red called over.

Trey turned and looked at her. She pointed at the big screen. It went blank then a confusing group of pictures sprayed across it. In each one Trey stared intently at something directly in front of him. "These are the pictures we have of Trey through the dogbots. As we thought, someone was tracking him, but with no order to apprehend."

"That's why we left you waiting for so long. We wanted to see who was following you. Unfortunately, it was just a regular police patrol." The Chief rolled himself over the computer screen.

"I think we know who was tracking him now." Red tapped a couple keys, and Trey saw his face replaced by a file picture. "You have friends in low places."

"I've never seen him before."

"I am not surprised. People who see this man find their lives changed, usually not for the better. All I have on him is that he is a Methuselah. His name's Joe. If he's looking for you, then your life is going to get very interesting. I'd really like to know what has two Methuselahs hunting you. The rumors say Grant and Joe don't like each other, but it won't help you if you're caught." The Chief looked hard at Trey. "We weren't planning to put you out on contract anyway since your face is very recognizable to people who know what to look for, but now I think we'll put you with one of the teams. That gives you a reason to stay out of general population. I would be happier if only a few people knew about you."

"I could use him on my team, Chief," Red spun away from the computer to look at Trey. "We're short."

"Are you sure?"

"He's cool. I explained the rules to him, and I'll talk with her."

"OK then, he's all yours." The Chief looked at Trey, his eyes still concerned.

The Youth are Revolting

Joe sat at his desk studying reports from the local police. One of them was from the crew who had shown up at an old underpass in response to a very faint nano signal. Several dogbots had seen Trey, but without definite orders to apprehend him, they had flagged the location and continued with their patrol.

Joe had dispatched the patrol when a sniffer detected the possible presence of nanos. The sniffers were supremely more sensitive than the dogbots, but were so small a patrol had to follow up to make the arrest. Only this time, there was no arrest. The report said there might have been movement in the underpass, and it looked like the access cover had been moved. They found no other sign. Because of jurisdictional issues they couldn't enter the tunnels to investigate until several hours had passed. There was nothing there.

Joe added it to the pile of almost evidence and innuendo that pointed to an organized resistance.

He'd mentioned it to the Council, once. Half

the Council thought he was losing his touch and should be retired, the other half wanted to call in the army. It had taken hours of careful mediation and coloring the truth to get them to relax again and trust him with the continuing investigation. Through the following years he had gleaned bits and pieces - enough to convince him he was dealing with a serious group. After Maggie had commented about computer glitches, he had moved all his files to paper files in the locked drawer of his desk. He sighed and rubbed his eyes. He closed the report and placed it with the others at the back of the drawer.

He pulled out another file. This one held information from the police investigating the latest slaying of a retiree. Once again he'd turned out to be an abuser of children according to a folder of evidence left at the scene.

Joe pulled out the other files and spread their contents across his desk, double checking the facts of each one, making notes on a yellow pad. He'd done this before, but each time he learned a little more. The weapons were exceptionally sharp daggers or a similar blade. They weren't very long, but the wounds were placed with deadly purpose. There was never much blood, suggesting the blades weren't removed until after the victim's heart stopped beating.

The scenes were immaculately cleaned, which meant one person who had nerves of steel, or a team who came in to do a quick and thorough cleaning. Also there was the evidence left to point to the victims' illicit activities. It suggested more than a single person's resources. The two files were linked. He would bet anything on it.

Joe got up and walked around the office. He thought better on his feet. What if the resistance was deliberately targeting people in responsibility who had abusive relationships with children? How would they find their targets? People had died in states across the country. Such action needed a widespread and well-organized network. Their weakness was that, by their very nature, it would be difficult to place agents in government offices. Almost all government employees were chosen from the ranks of the near retirement-aged.

But they could have people from a broad cross section of the rest of society. The young were treated badly, and it was getting worse. An unhappy population would be a breeding ground for the kind of agents they needed. What better way to train killers than to start them off with people who deserved to die?

He sat down and buzzed for Maggie.

"I need the officers on these murders to go back through their interviews and check for the presence of children."

"Children?"

"I think the perpetrators are using children to gain access to their victims."

"Oh dear."

"Exactly."

Joe sat at his desk and reluctantly pulled out the keyboard and activated the screen. If the resistance was finding pedophiles; he should be able to follow their tracks. He typed in a random search then meandered through the morass of the internet.

It was still as unmanageable as it had been two centuries ago when it was first introduced. After eliminating all the sites hosted outside of the U.S. he still had more garbage than he wanted to wade through. The victims so far were actively involved in trafficking children. So he could screen out the sites "just" showing other sites' pictures. He set search bots on the remainder with commands to find people who showed up in more sites than the median. They would sift through the chat rooms as well. It wouldn't matter what the sign-in name was. The bots were programmed to look at the user's IP address. He requested the victim's IP addresses to add to the search.

Disgusted at the pictures on his screen, Joe pushed the keyboard away, and the screen retracted. Every time he thought he had a handle on human depravity, he was surprised again. He needed a change of view. Perhaps it was time to visit a Deputy Chancellor on his own turf. Joe was still curious about what the man was hiding. Picking up his cane, he left his office and let Maggie know where he was going.

***

Deputy Chancellor Muholland faced the delegation from the Union of East Pacific States. They danced diplomatically around the possibility of a trade agreement. Fortunately, those countries respected age. Unfortunately, that respect didn't actually translate into any kind of advantage. Their reverence for age was counterbalanced by a hard-headed certainty the future belonged to the young. The aged were supposed to step aside and be founts of wisdom.

When his secretary knocked discreetly and indicated an agent from the Methuselahs was waiting outside, the D.C. had a hard time hiding his relief as he apologetically bowed the delegation out of his office. He told the secretary to make sure they had a full schedule for the next few days so he could catch his breath.

****

Joe followed D.C. Mulholland into his office, a very different room than Joe's. It spoke of ambition and political power.

"Welcome, sir."

"Please just call me Joe." He settled himself carefully in a chair. Mulholland closed the outer door, and sat in a chair he pulled over to face Joe's.

"Any news?" Mulholland leaned forward.

"It appears Trey has managed to disappear without a trace. I put some feelers out, but I need to be careful. The people who are going to be looking for him are just as careful as I am and I don't want to tip my hand. I think he had help disappearing. Now, I'm searching for the people who helped him rather than Trey himself. Do you have any ideas about who they might be?" Joe leaned back a little in the chair and held his cane in front of him.

"I can't say for certain. There are a number of criminal organizations who would have the resources to make someone vanish." He shook his head. "I can't think of why they would want to get involved. There is no monetary value in holding Trey. His value is purely political." Mulholland slumped in his seat as if he'd lost some air.

Joe waited silently without moving. The Deputy Chancellor was holding back. Joe was sure of it, and it had something to do with Trey. D.C. Mulholland showed no signs of revealing anything more, just slumped in his chair, looking defeated.

Joe excused himself as the secretary came pushing a cart with coffee. Maggie's timing wouldn't have been so far off.

As he rode the car back to the office, Joe considered what he'd been told. Nothing new, yet it solidified his hunch Trey was not an ordinary young man.

When he got back to his office, another Methuselah waited from him in the hall.

"Hello, Grant." Joe raised an eyebrow. "Slumming it now, are you?"

"You were visiting Deputy Chancellor Mulholland. Why?" Grant's voice was as cold as his eyes.

"I had some questions to ask him about a case."

"About a young man who appears to have vanished from a Youth Reserve." It was a statement not a question.

"He asked me to look into it. I was telling him I had no results from my search, and asking who might have profited from his disappearance. He couldn't say."

"It is my case. Stay out of it." Grant stood up. "Deputy Chancellor Mulholland made a mistake once. I want to be sure he doesn't repeat it."

"Why is this Trey so important? Mulholland wouldn't be the first retiree to have a late comer child."

"He isn't just a late comer. We have good reason to think the boy is a clone of Mulholland."

"The genetic tests..."

"Are inconclusive. He isn't genetically identical, but he is closer than he should be. We suspect Mulholland is behind the disappearance. I am sure further testing will show he is in need of a transplant. Trey would be the logical donor."

"Why not just do the testing?"

"He's a retiree. Mulholland has rights, and my certainty of his guilt is not evidence. He's being watched. Stay away from him, Joe." He turned and walked away.

A clone. Interesting. Especially since the lad is well into his teens, and no clone had ever survived past the age of ten. That suggested some intriguing possibilities. Grant always did show his cards too soon, though Joe wasn't about to underestimate him.

He went into his office and thought about clones, age and politics.

TRAINING EXERCISES

The subject of Joe's cogitation was being chased by five teens with paint ball guns. He ducked behind a wall and caught his breath. Red's idea of training was to turn him loose in the tunnels and then hunt him down. He had a limited time to find his way to an arbitrary safe zone. Half the time Trey didn't even know how to get to the safe zone. Bruises and welts covered him from head to toe.

He'd learned to avoid most of the team, but Lizzy always found him. She took special delight in gunning him down. Never one shot, but at least half a dozen. The rest of the team just shrugged. He was the new kid, and they didn't know him well enough to be sympathetic. Even Red said he'd have to figure it out.

Trey sat with his back in a corner of a deserted room watching the door. *Where the Hell am I? I'm tired of this game.* The safe zone might as well have been on the other side of the world for all the good it did him. For the first few days after he arrived, Trey's mind might as well have been packed with cotton balls, but now it was sharp as it had ever been.

I need to change the rules of the game. He created a map in his head of all the places they had trained. It was far from complete, but it did allow him to figure out his probable location, and more importantly where the rest of the team would be. He slipped out of the room and headed back toward some stairs. Jimmy was the most predictable of the team. He liked coming at Trey from above.

Time for a surprise.

Trey quieted his breathing and listened. A telltale scuffing came from around a corner. Jimmy always dragged his feet. Trey smiled, then crouched low and waited for the other boy to come closer. He picked up a small piece of concrete and skipped it down the corridor. As he had hoped, Jimmy leapt around the corner with his gun at the ready. Trey grabbed Jimmy's arm, pulled him off balance and took the gun from him. Trey pointed the gun at him.

"Surrender or I shoot, and let me tell you, these things hurt at this range." Jimmy raised his hands. "Now hand me your equipment." It made an impressive pile. Trey took the walkie-talkie and the extra paintballs. The rest he pushed back to Jimmy. "Let's go." He waggled the gun and made Jimmy walk in front of him.

Listening to the radio he could hear the rest of the group closing in. Just as they came to a cross tunnel Jimmy yelled out. Trey grabbed his shoulder and pulled him to the wall. The first person came around the corner gun blazing, but this time they hit

Jimmy, who shouted in anger. Trey fired over his prisoner's shoulder and tagged the first and the second person to charge. Annie and Bert were both down.

Now the team knew something was up. Trey swung Jimmy around just as Red slipped through a utility door behind him. Once again Jimmy took the brunt of the shots. Trey emptied his gun toward his team leader. He thought he hit her twice. Trey didn't wait to find out. He dashed around the corner, ducking and weaving to avoid shots from behind in case his shots hadn't been 'fatal'. He came to a door standing slightly ajar. He almost pushed through it to escape the team behind him. *Doors are never left open by accident.*

Likely Lizzy was waiting for him to come crashing through and present a target. The radio chatter had stopped with Red informing her team they were all dead and shut up about it. *That answered that question.* It was down to him, Lizzy and Dan. Lizzy almost never spoke over the radio, so she wasn't likely to give up her position. She knew he was armed, but he didn't think that would stop her. He needed to outmaneuver her.

After reloading his gun, Trey walked quickly down the tunnel and made a left. He continued to the next junction and turned left there as well. He hoped the next turn would put him back in the original corridor, but a little ways up. Sure enough when he peeked around the next corner he could see his disgruntled opponents sitting in the tunnel talking. They weren't looking his way so he slipped across the corridor. After another left, the group he'd already taken out was between him and where he thought Lizzy had set up. Now he just needed a way to draw her out. He sat down with his back to the wall so he could see down the tunnels three ways. It was time to find out how patient she was.

He figured it was about half an hour when he heard the scrape from the tunnel behind him. It would be either Lizzy or Dan, and probably Dan. The "dead" members of the team sat dejectedly at the corner. Jimmy looked toward where Trey was hidden, and brightened. He made a move to wave and Red pointed her finger like a gun at him. But it gave Trey an idea. He whispered into the radio.

"Watch behind you." Hearing another scrape he rolled out into the corridor. Not Dan, Lizzy just completed a full circle. He fired three shots, each one hitting her torso. He finished his roll into the corridor and pressed himself against the wall. He heard a strange sound from behind him, but he finally identified it. Lizzy was laughing. He walked to the almost-closed door and told Dan he could surrender or wait until they all starved. Dan came out with a grin on his face.

After that exercise, the group began to accept Trey as one of their own. They also started to explore what Trey had to offer their group. Each had an area of expertise.

Trey had seen Red hacking the dogbot network when he'd met the Chief. Trey could use a computer well enough, but what Red did might as well have been magic. She worked the group on more basic hacking maneuvers, especially how to hijack security systems.

"Our best friend is the target's security system once we own it. Instead of alerting them to our presence, it tells us how many people are present and where they are." She had them hacking into networks she created. "No security software will warn you if you're busted, so you need to be aware of what is going on in the background. Sudden movement around the target is a danger sign. But don't forget to watch your physical location for danger."

Dan was their instructor in unarmed combat.

"Let's warm up with a few punches," Dan stood in sweat pants and torn t-shirt in the room they used for training. "Fifty each side, count them off."

Dan left Red counting punches at high speed and came to watch Trey.

"Pull your hand back to your waist, like so." He moved Trey's hand. "When you punch your hand twists to strike with the two largest knuckles."

Trey'd never given punching much thought, other than how not to be the target for someone else. He finished the fifty just as the others completed fifty blocks.

Dan broke them into pairs. Trey wanted Red, but she made a beeline for Dan so he got Jimmy instead.

"Slow motion, no contact. One punch, one block, then switch."

Jimmy's first punch blew past Trey's attempt at a block. It landed just below his solar plexus and made him grunt. He tried to breathe and get back in the ready stance, but his lungs wouldn't cooperate.

Dan came over and put his hand on Trey's shoulder.

"Breathe slower."

He stood in front of Jimmy.

"Let's try it again."

Trey expected Dan to clobber Jimmy and from the expression on the smaller boy's face he expected it too. Instead Dan moved with glacial slowness and forced Jimmy to match him. They stayed with it while Red got the rest of the group working on kicks. When Trey looked over briefly, Dan hadn't broken a sweat, but Jimmy looked like he was ready to drop.

"Enough," Dan walked back his spot at the front. "Remember, control is power. If you control yourself completely, you control your opponent.

Dan invited Trey to bunk with him instead of the temporary room. Trey slept better with the sound of another person breathing in his room.

Trey collected a new set of bruises as he learned the basic skills. Like Red's game, the unarmed combat training consisted of the other team members throwing him around, then Dan showing him what he did wrong. For all his size and ferocity in the combat training, he had an ever-present smile. A little unnerving when Trey ducked and wove away from a flurry of kicks and punches, or worse when Dan would reach down to pull Trey to his feet, informing him he was dead. Again. Jimmy never partnered with him if he didn't have to.

"What does Lizzy do while we're thumping each other?" Trey rolled to his feet yet again. Dan was trying to teach him a leg sweep.

"She has her own training, but it wouldn't be safe for her to work with us here."

"C'mon, nobody would hurt her."

"That's not the issue," Dan swept Trey's legs out from under him, then offered his hand to help him up. "She's afraid she'll hurt one of us."

Trey caught the absolute seriousness of Dan's expression, so he rolled to his feet and let the topic drop. Though he didn't understand how someone who looked no more than eight could be as dangerous as everyone said. Lizzy treated him like she did all the others in the group apart from Red, which meant she tolerated him as a nuisance.

***

One afternoon, Jimmy sidled up beside Trey.

"Hey, you. Up for some fun?"

Trey put his mostly empty cup on the tray and carried it over to the rack. Maybe he could do something about the wall between him and Jimmy.

They climbed up the stairs to the upper floor. Jimmy led the way to a hallway of doors.

"Not all the doors we need to get through will be unlocked." He opened a backpack Trey hadn't noticed and pulled out a black cloth. It unrolled to reveal a strange assortment of tools and electronic gadgets. "This is how we get in. I don't expect you to get past the fancy locks, but you should be able to pick a basic one."

He handed Trey a long thin flat piece of metal

and a finer round one.

"This is how it's done." He knelt beside one of the doors and slid in the flat piece, then the round one and in seconds he had the door open.

"You try."

Trey tried to copy the exact motions Jimmy'd made, but the door stayed stubbornly locked.

"You have to feel for it. You want to push the tumblers out of the way."

Trey knelt at the door fumbling with the picks until suddenly something moved. He got the next one faster and soon had the door open.

"Not bad for a novice, though the cops would have come and dragged you away long ago."

They worked on a few more doors and Trey got marginally faster.

"Practice," Jimmy told him. "Keep the picks with you. You never know when you want them. Trey put the picks beneath the insole of his shoe and practiced when he had the chance. He wanted to impress Jimmy next time he had a chance.

Trey didn't know what Annie and Bert's roles were. They were easy going and friendly. Each of them took turns sparring with Trey during training, or showing him around the Underground. They never answered any direct questions.

Bert apparently was in charge of meals for the team. They ate in a room with a table and lockers for gear that didn't fit in their rooms. Comments about the food were leveled at Bert. The oldest person on the team, Bert might have been Harry's age, but he'd grin at complaints and list the strange or horrible things the team might find on their plates next meal.

The Chief rolled through their training at odd times. Hand to hand combat against a trained opponent in a wheelchair was much harder than Trey imagined. Occasionally the Chief ate with them, and once caught Trey trying to pick a lock on a door up on the balcony over the Underground.

"You want to watch your back, Trey." The Chief grinned wryly. "The security people aren't thrilled with people breaking into locked rooms. They aren't as gentle as I am."

Once Trey had mapped the tunnels in his head, he tried to put them on paper sitting at the table in the team's dining room. Drawing a map in three dimensions would have been hard even if he could draw. He left in disgust to find a roll of exquisitely detailed maps on the table the next day with a note from the Chief.

Trey never met any other teams, and rarely did more than say hello to anyone outside his own.

The training was one of the best times of Trey's life. He belonged in a way he'd never imagined possible. They were all different, so no one was more of an outsider than any other. Though Red didn't treat him any differently than the rest of the team, Trey couldn't get enough time in her company.

The six team members trained and ate together daily, but other than a general agreement that the present system wasn't fair, none of them talked about why they were part of the underground. Trey got his first lesson in underground politics when Red announced they had an assignment.

First Action

Red gathered them in the small room they used for their briefings. Instead of the maps and tasks for the day, she had posted pictures and charts. There was none of her usual banter.

"We have an assignment today. The target is charged with crimes against children. The evidence is before you. Familiarize yourself with the case and we will talk about it."

Trey went up with the others and looked at the pictures. They horrified him. They showed an adult with his face blacked out abusing several different children in ways that made his stomach knot up. Nobody, especially not a kid should be sacrificed for someone else's pleasure. The others were just as angry, but no one said anything except an occasional profanity. Trey wanted to hit something. He breathed the way Dan taught them and separated his emotion from his need to think and analyze.

Some charts showed time lines of the person's dealings with children identified as the ones in the picture. Other charts detailed how the perpetrator was uncovered. There were statements from victims and their families, security footage and phone taps, and reports from investigators. When they sat at the table again, Red passed around some files. They contained statements from children listing the abuse its effect on them. What puzzled Trey was the name of the accused was blacked out.

"Now you've seen the case, what is your verdict?"

"Guilty."

"Guilty."

"Guilty."

"Guilty."

"May I ask a question for clarification?" asked Trey.

"Go ahead." Red tapped her file with a finger, but her face didn't reflect any impatience with his questions.

"I am assuming you know who the person is. Why have they not been identified?"

"We do everything we can to avoid bias. Most of the cases involve people who are recognizable through their position. We don't want that to influence the evidence in front of us. So the identity of the accused is hidden until the verdict is rendered."

"Another question. Why are we discussing this? Why not the police?"

"Crimes against children are growing as more and more Olders see children as things, not people. The police priorities reflect the priorities of the government, and many of the people we deal with are government."

"What Red is saying is the police don't care about kids. So, if these freaks are going to be stopped, then we need to do the stopping." Jimmy banged the table and glared at Trey.

"Then I would agree this person is guilty."

Red nodded and went to the computer in the corner of the room. After a moment she returned.

"The other tribunals have also returned a verdict of guilty." She turned to Trey. "We hold three simultaneous tribunals to review the evidence. Each one must return a guilty verdict for us to proceed. There is one from the Middlers, people over sixty, one from a random group drawn from the market, and the team. We are included because we carry out the sentence, and we need to be absolutely sure we are doing right thing."

The others looked serious and nodded at Trey.

"If you aren't sure, now is the time to back out," Dan said.

"I'd like to kill the sick bastard," Trey restrained himself. He could understand Jimmy hammering the table.

"Very good, because that's exactly what we are going to do." Lizzy smiled at Trey. Though she wore jeans and a t-shirt looking even younger than usual, he felt cold in the pit of his stomach. It was not a friendly smile.

"Planning then," Red dropped some files on the table and everyone picked one up. "Here's what we have so far. He has the habit of getting his victims from a panderer who works out of a shelter. We are going to pick him up at there. We will need to find a way to get Lizzy into place, because this one doesn't pick up random children. That means hitting the panderer and convincing him to cooperate. We haven't built a complete case against him yet, so we tag him and turn him loose.

"Dan, you and Jimmy are going to hit the panderer, you will have Lizzy with you so try to stay on track. Trey, you will go with Annie and Bert. You'll be on clean up. I'll give you the location to wait for Lizzy's call. As usual we maintain complete communications silence until Lizzy calls for cleanup. I will be monitoring and give backup as needed. Clear?"

"Clear," the team said.

The team stood up and the two groups took equipment from a cupboard. Red watched them make their selections. She paid special attention to Trey. He took a jacket a bit too large for him and a hat to cover his red hair. There wasn't much he could do about his face, but Red passed him a pair of sunglasses. Annie and Bert told him they kept a pack with everything they needed, adding to it as they learned new tricks.

Lizzy wore a wig over her hair and had colored her eyebrows. Contact lenses tinted her eyes brown. Trey wouldn't have recognized her if he hadn't watched the transformation.

Soon they followed Red and Dan through the tunnels up to a large garage filled with vehicles. Red handed a map to Bert. The cleanup crew piled into a beat up van while the others climbed into a sedan, and headed into town.

Annie and Bert filled Trey in on what would be happening at the shelter.

"Red'll drop them at a corner near the shelter. Dan and Jimmy will circle to the back while Lizzy heads to the front door putting on a helpless face. There are always kids showing up at these places. I used to work at one and it ate away at me until I had to do something about it.

"With luck the panderer will be working tonight. He's a janitor, not subject to the same fine scrutiny as the other employees since he has no contact with the occupants."

"Lizzy will make herself comfortable, while Jimmy and Dan break in the back and find a safe room to wait." Bert parked the van in an alley. "This is the meeting point.

Trey read the file they had collected on the panderer. The people running this shelter had turned cynical. They generated terrific numbers- the envy of every other shelter in the city, but also turned a blind eye to staff running side businesses out of the shelter. The primary concern was to keep the moonlighting from interfering with the efficient and profitable management of the shelter.

The nature of the shelter made it easy for the janitor to ingratiate himself into the trust of the staff. His cleaning routine gave him complete access to the shelter records. No one questioned it because no money ever went missing. What he looked for was more insidious. He watched for children to come in with a lack of attachments and supports who would fit his clients' rather particular needs.

Lizzy would catch his eye. She was completely alone; the kind of child who came in and out of the shelter on a daily basis as they learned to play the system. He would make sure she felt special. Maybe give her clothes or other treats. Trey felt ill as he put the file down. He didn't think of the Youth Reserve as a sheltered upbringing, but it hadn't prepared him for evil like this.

Jimmy slipped into the van a half hour later.

"You should have seen it," he said. "It was priceless. The guy brought her to the exact room where Dan and I waited. He tried to buy her with clothes. 'These are nicer than what you have on,' he says. 'Try them on.' The moron didn't even notice we were there. Lizzy held up the clothes for us and asked which we liked. 'The pink makes you look sickly," Dan said, 'Better wear the green.' I thought the old guy was going to die on the spot. He makes like he was going to run for it, but Lizzy took him down. 'We need him alive, for now.' Dan said, not even looking at the guy."

"So did the guy give you what you need?" Bert asked.

"Oh sure, he coughed up the meeting place for the guy we're after and tried to buy us off with some other information."

"Substantiated?"

"He didn't have anything in writing. He seemed to be terrified of the people he was ratting out. I don't think he's got a great life expectancy."

"Any names we know?"

"A couple we have our eyes on, and one new name that will give the Chief six kinds of fits."

"So who would scare the Chief?

"How about Councilman Molloy?

Trey just stared at Jimmy along with Bert and Annie. Councilman Molloy, the chair of the Council of Elders, was at least two hundred years old.

"Are you sure?"

"The guy wet his pants just saying the name. There's no doubt he's scared."

"Red needs to hear about this, immediately," Annie said.

"Let's stay on task," Bert said. "We have a job to do. We don't break communications silence."

They watched the back of the shelter until Lizzy came out with Dan who had dressed in the janitor's clothes. She fastidiously mopped her hands with a cloth which she tossed into a garbage pile. Dan rolled his eyes as he walked past the van while Lizzy skipped ahead. Trey had a hard time believing this innocent child was the same Lizzy who trained with them and took a special pleasure in bruising him with her paintball gun as much as Red would allow.

"Oh great," Bert said, "he must have pissed her off. Jimmy, you and Trey go check it out. Do what you can to clean up."

Trey slipped out the back of the van and followed Jimmy to the door into the shelter. A man lay on the floor of the cluttered room. Trey could smell the urine and vomit, though it didn't look as if there was any blood. He could hear the man's rasping breathing. Bruises were beginning to show on his face and from the way he curled in a fetal position, Trey was sure Lizzy had given him at least one good blow to the groin. The man groaned and Trey waved Jimmy out of the man's sight.

"Listen," Trey tried to make his voice lower and rougher, "you got beat up by some punks who used a kid to get into the shelter to rob it. They've run off, and you're going to be a hero."

"Quit," said the man choking and puking up some more.

"You can't quit, can you?" Trey nudged him with his toe. "There are people who depend on you, who will be very disappointed if you try to run." The man on the floor stiffened then started shaking. "That's right, you should be afraid. Too late for you to do anything, but what we tell you. We'll be in touch." Trey stood up and walked out the door with Jimmy following him.

"What do you think you were doing?" Jimmy said in a hiss as soon as the door closed behind them.

"We need him," Trey said. "He's the only link we have to find out if Councilor Molloy really is dirty."

"You as much as told him there were people watching him. What if he tries to trade that to Molloy? We don't need the Geris knowing about us."

"It's a sure thing they know we exist. We can put a team in the shelter to keep an eye on him. We need him alive and in place to get to Molloy."

"Damn, damn, damn," Jimmy said, "I don't like this." He climbed into the van and threw himself into a seat. "We need to talk to the Chief."

"When this mission is done," Bert said, "we'll all be talking to the Chief." A beep sounded from the front of the van. "There's our cue. Lizzy is with the target. It's time to move."

He started up the van and drove through streets filled with Youngers. Their eyes looked hopeless. These people knew even if by some chance they made it to retirement, the Home was the only thing waiting for them. The streets gradually emptied and became more respectable. Bert followed a beeping dot on a screen in front of him. When they arrived at the source, it wasn't Lizzy, but Dan who waited for them, leaning against a light post.

"What did you do with the body?" he asked as soon as the door was closed. Jimmy looked at Trey.

"The bastard is still breathing," he said. "Trey, here, had a bright idea."

Dan just looked at Trey and raised an eyebrow.

"We need him alive," Trey said. "If Councilor Molloy really is dirty, the janitor's the only connection we have."

Dan shook his head, but just turned to Bert.

"Head down this street and take the second left. There's a store we can park at where we'll be less conspicuous while we wait for Lizzy's signal."

Once at the store, Annie went in to 'shop' while Bert made a show of tapping his fingers on the steering wheel. Trey and the others sat far enough back as to be invisible to a casual observer. Annie came out the store just as Bert's phone rang.

"It's done." He put the van into gear. In a few minutes they pulled into a side street. Red was already there with the sedan. Bert looked at Trey.

"Go," he said, "You need to see this."

Trey swallowed and slipped out of the van and joined Red in the car. She drove down a few more streets before pulling into a driveway.

"Grab the briefcase from the trunk," she said.

Trey picked up the case and followed her to the door. At some point while they'd waited she'd changed into a tailored suit making her look older and harder. The door opened to her knock, and she led Trey into the house. Lizzy wore a body suit the same color as her skin. She ignored the little blood on her and carefully inspected her knives, running her fingers along the blades.

"What's he doing here?" She pointed a knife at Trey.

"Same as always, Lizzy," Red answered. "We need a witness to confirm the execution"

Lizzy shrugged and led them down the hall to a room where a body lay on its back. The man was naked from the waist down, there was some blood on his shirt but not as much as Trey would have imagined. He could smell urine from the doorway. Red took the case from him and opened it up. She handed Lizzy a set of clothes and left a file folder on the dresser.

"We're finished," she said and led them out into the foyer. She gave the door knob a final wipe and left the door not quite closed. The three climbed into the car and drove off. Trey never saw the van, though it pulled into the garage only seconds after Red parked.

"Time to go home," she said, and led Trey through a door down into the tunnels.

FINDING TROUBLE

Trey looked at his team as they waited in the Chief's office. Red sat at the computer running searches and trying to get more information on the possibility Councilor Molloy was committing crimes against children. Lizzy sat and tapped her fingers on the desk beside her. She might as well have been blind and deaf for all the attention she paid to the rest of the team. Bert massaged Annie's shoulders and occasionally bent over to whisper something in her ear. A couple of times she smiled. Jimmy alternated between throwing himself in a sprawl on one of the chairs, only to jump up and look over Red's shoulder or talk to Dan who appeared to have fallen asleep standing up in the corner. Trey put the team out of his mind and concentrated on the events of the day.

"Chief, Trey let the janitor know there were people watching him. He should have been killed."

Trey looked up. The Chief's face looked carved from stone. Silence was his best plan at this point.

"We never intended to kill him, Jimmy," the Chief said. "We don't have a complete file on him."

"But he's a danger to us!"

"Perhaps, but we don't kill people for knowing about us. He's not been convicted of crimes against children."

"I don't care if he's supplying children to Molloy, but what if he talks about us?"

"What if he does? You knew it was part of the risk."

"But --"

"Are you asking to be removed from the team?"

"No, but --"

"There are no buts, Jimmy. Either you work by the rules or you're out."

"I'm in." The energy seemed to go out of Jimmy, and he slumped into a chair. "You'll want to hear from the new kid."

"Trey?" The Chief looked at him.

"I left the panderer at the shelter with the impression his employers were still very interested in him continuing his...work. Some of the information he gave Jimmy and Dan was important enough to risk leaving him in place."

"The information?"

"He talked to us about the important people he expected to protect him, " Dan said from the corner, "...must have thought it would impress us. One of the names he mentioned was Councilor Molloy."

"That *is* interesting," the Chief said, "and disturbing."

"It makes sense if you look at it politically." Trey set the gnawing in his gut aside to speak clearly. He silently thanked Hank at the Reserve for the inadvertent training in keeping a cool head. "The Elders have all but made it illegal to be young. Anyone under retirement age is virtually an indentured slave with no rights to organize, criticize the government or anything else which might upset the balance of power. Given those attitudes, it is inevitable some of the people in power would view the young, and especially children as things rather than human beings. Even those who suspect would turn a blind eye, because to care too much about the young might be seen as treason against the ruling powers."

"So the Council thinks it's all right to kill children?" Jimmy asked.

"They would try very hard to not think about it at all," Trey ground his teeth to keep his voice even. "I'm assuming that's why you leave the file with the evidence of wrongdoing at the scene so the police will see what is happening. Has it made any difference yet?"

"No." Red spun around to join the conversation. "Nobody has picked it up. We send information to the news services, and it gets ignored there too."

"I am guessing any web sites you set up to disseminate the information tend to crash quickly as well."

Red nodded and spun back to the computer.

"The evidence points to a person or a group in a position of power who doesn't want the information getting out. They may not be in direct collusion with the people abusing children, but they are going to do their best to keep the situation under wraps." Trey unclenched his hands from the table. This was dangerously close to the kind of thing leading to beatings at the Reserve.

"So what do you suggest?" Jimmy jumped up and started pacing again, waving his hands wildly. "Just let them win?"

"Chief, how many executions has this team carried out?" Trey tried to fit the pieces into a clear picture in his head.

"Six, including today," the Chief said.

"Seven," Lizzy said. "There were two at one house."

"Thank you, Lizzy. Seven executions. Before you ask, the other teams across the country don't have as many executions to their credit, but it is still a substantial number over all."

"Yet it is nowhere near the number of people who actually hurt children. Our actions are meant to be political, not preventive." Red spoke without taking her eyes from the computer.

"Every pervert we take out is one less to hurt children!" Jimmy said.

"True, but the main response needs to be political, or we would be doing nothing but killing people all day." The Chief rubbed his temples.

"What's wrong with that?" Lizzy said.

"It would corrupt us and turn us into murderers instead of revolutionaries." The Chief looked over at Lizzy.

She shrugged and looked away.

"Suggestions?" the Chief asked.

"I would suggest we concentrate on Councilor

Molloy, and see where it takes us." Trey caught Red's startled look. *Great, I'm getting her angry too.* "If he's the one who is stonewalling you, removing him could also remove the roadblocks to the political action you want." Bits and pieces joined and broke up in his head. He couldn't get a clear idea of what he needed next.

The Chief looked around at the team then nodded.

"You'd better get to it then."

Red pushed away from the keyboard and walked out of the room. Dan followed close behind. Trey waited until they'd all left. The Chief raised an eyebrow so Trey hustled to catch up. Red led them to the deserted hallways where they did their training.

"Run. Five miles to start." She dashed off at high speed and Trey put everything aside except for the need to keep up.

***

By the time Trey finished the run he was exhausted. The last mile he'd had to concentrate to put one foot in front of the other. He was the last to stagger in, but the rest of the team slapped his back and joked with him. Somehow in five miles they had put whatever troubled them aside and become a team again.

"We talk in twenty minutes. Showers first." Red wrinkled her nose at Trey and winked. His heart lifted a bit. Maybe she'd forgiven him.

***

The pictures and charts on the briefing room wall were gone when Trey got back, a little refreshed from the show. The others paced or lounged in chairs. Red came in and walked to the front of the room.

"You know why we're here," she said without preamble. "I talked to the Chief, we have permission to use whatever resources we need to investigate the Councilor. As of this moment Councilor Molloy is our only concern."

"What about other executions?" Lizzy asked.

"They will be handled by another team."

Lizzy looked as if she wanted to say something more, but she just settled back and crossed her arms.

"You could ask for a transfer to another team," Red said her voice as gentle as Trey'd ever heard it.

"I work with you. No one else."

"Well that's nice. I thought we were all part of the team," Jimmy said. Lizzy stared at him and Jimmy whitened then looked back at Red. "So now what, oh fearless leader?"

"We need to keep an eye on the janitor at the shelter. He hasn't met Annie yet. I thought Annie could go in with Bert as a backup."

"I could be a volunteer," Annie said. "I've done it before."

Red nodded, and looked at Jimmy.

"You want to feel out your contacts on the street? Don't mention any names, but they may know if someone with that kind of power is taking advantage of their services."

Jimmy nodded and looked at his shoes. "Can I take something to grease the wheels?"

"Keep it reasonable...and nothing which can be traced to us."

84

"Trey, can you think of anything else?" Red looked at him, along with the rest of the team.

"We need to be looking for patterns. Are there similar disappearances or deaths around about the time the Councilor is in town? They might have been chosen as much as a month in advance and dumped some time afterward. Look especially for similar kinds of injuries."

Red made a couple of notes, and looked at Dan and Lizzy.

"I don't have anything for you yet, just stay sharp."

Dan nodded and Lizzy just stared.

"Well then, team, let's get to it. We want to bring this Molloy down or prove he's clean, and whichever way it goes, I don't want to take a lot of time with it." The team got up and left. Trey saw Lizzy and Red in a heated discussion as the door closed behind him.

He'd worked hard to be part of the team. Time to make it count. Trey sighed, would he ever get to stop being just a brain?

Separate Issues

Maggie stormed into Joe's office and slammed a pile of files on his desk. His coffee cup jumped and spilled. He pushed back to avoid being splashed by the hot black liquid. She frowned at him then stomped back out of the office. Joe sighed and mopped up the mess with his handkerchief. Maggie hadn't talked to him in days and hadn't smiled in much longer.

He'd made a mistake asking her to research the people involved in trafficking children. Maggie was a much better researcher than he was, but she expected him to rush out and fix every new situation she uncovered. As he eliminated them from his list of possible targets for one reason or another he would send a note to the local police force, but that wasn't enough for her.

Swamped under stacks of depravity, Joe despaired of finding a way to deal with the problem. Even if only a small fraction of the retiree population acted as if children were toys to be purchased, broken, and replaced, there were still far too many. It revolted him. He felt like a monster for focusing only on cases potentially leading him closer to the shadowy organization opposing the government.

The worst part was in certain cases Joe had found notes forbidding any further investigation. Those notes had turned Maggie into this raging dragon. She wanted Joe to focus specifically on those cases. Joe had refused. Even a Methuselah had limits on his powers. The person who put those notes on the case files did not.

Joe opened his desk and looked at the half dozen files in black folders. He was taking a huge risk just by keeping them. *Well, no guts, no glory*. He buzzed Maggie.

"Maggie, would you step in here, please."

The door slammed open and the dragon came and stood at attention in front of his desk. Her eyes widened when she saw the black folders in his hand.

"Methuselah Roberta has been talking about quitting; some nonsense about the work not having any meaning. Please send all this..." a wave of his hand took in all the ragged piles on his desk and floor "...with my compliments. When you have finished, I would like you to join me for lunch."

Maggie's eyes widened again then narrowed. She nodded and left the office. A few minutes later someone in blue coveralls came in with some boxes and a dolly. Joe paid little attention as he quickly and efficiently boxed up the hundreds of files without a glance at any of the contents.

Joe spread the six black files on his desk. What was the link between these individuals? They weren't the worst offenders. There were files on the way up to

Roberta's office that gave him nightmares. These people didn't abuse children. They bought and sold them, not in trailer loads, but in ones or twos. They didn't live in one place, but were scattered across the country. None of them was powerful. None was even close to retirement age. It wasn't who they were. It had to be about who they were serving. Someone wanted these people protected. They wanted to be able to buy children conveniently.

"Maggie." He said through the intercom. "It's time for lunch." He picked up his cane and carried the files through the door into Maggie's office. He dropped them into the shredder on the way past. He flashed her a hand sign and indicated the door. They went out to the elevator.

"I am very sorry I have been working you so hard. It is so easy to get caught up in my cases." Joe kept up the apologetic patter all the way to the lobby and out the doors of the Elder Justice building. He even meant most of it.

"What's this about Joe?" Maggie's voice was colder than the wind blowing the drizzle into their faces.

"We cannot investigate those black files without setting off alarms somewhere. So we are going to drop those files. Roberta will go through the rest like a terrier through a pack of rats." Joe glanced around. No one was close to them, and long range listeners wouldn't work well in the rain. "We are going after the person who put the "Do not investigate" tags on the black files. It is going to be the most dangerous investigation we have ever done. If you want to leave I will understand."

"I do want to leave, but not because of the risk. These cases have gotten under my skin. I keep looking at people in Justice and wonder if they're the ones who are protecting those...slavers. I watch the politics and the pettiness, and wonder if it is worth getting older. I can't do this anymore." She wiped her eyes. "I didn't know how to tell you without you blaming yourself. I can't do this anymore."

Joe walked a ways in stunned silence. The rain was hardly colder than his gut. Did he deserve to live as long as he had? All around him were people who saw only one reality in life. Were you a retiree or not? That artificial line had become the testing point of the value of human life. If you were eighty you were a valuable citizen, if not you were only slightly better off than a mediaeval peasant.

"If I were a hundred years younger, I would join the revolt myself."

Maggie looked at him for a long time.

"You don't look that old."

"There are...treatments for those who can afford them - one of the perks of being a Methuselah. We can't afford to have everyone live out retirement in luxury and leisure. Someone has to run the country. Unfortunately I'm no longer sure our selection criteria are any use at all."

They walked in silence the rest of the way to the restaurant. There, they shook out their coats while the owner fussed over them. Lunch was delicious, but awkward. Joe had planned to strategize, but Maggie's announcement had thrown him for a loop.

He tried to make small talk, but felt like a Younger on a first date. When lunch was done he paid, and called a cab to take them back through the now pouring rain. The driver insisted on holding an umbrella over them as they climbed the steps. Joe and Maggie were silent down to the basement.

"Good bye, Joe." She said as they reached her office. "It really has been great working with you. Don't let this last week spoil it."

"What are you going to do now?"

"I bought a club. You know the one. Come down and see me sometime." She kissed him on the lips then turned away.

Joe trudged with a heavy heart to his office and let himself in. He spent the afternoon pretending to work.

***

Towards evening there was a quiet knock on the door and a Younger let himself in.

"Ms. Mae told me you needed a new assistant with some of my skills."

"And what skills would they be?"

"Very discreet computer searches, an ability to think for myself."

"Do you have your papers?" Joe put out his hand.

The Younger, who might have been fifty at most, pulled out a wallet and passed over a couple of cards. Joe keyed up his computer and swiped the cards. Sure enough Devon had sufficient clearance and proficiency to work at this level – unusual in someone so young, but he did come with Maggie's recommendation.

"We will give it a try for a while. Get yourself set up outside. I will give you some instructions tomorrow."

The next day Devon stood quietly in the office while Joe stumped around him, peering at him from all sides. Finally Joe sat down behind his desk and waved the younger man to a seat. Devon was slim and dressed professionally. A faint scent clung to him, but nothing Joe could identify. Something about him piqued Joe's curiosity. He stomped it down. It wouldn't do to start a new working relationship with a feeling of mistrust. He didn't know Devon, but he'd trust Maggie with his life.

"I find the older I get, the harder it is to deal with changes that affect my comfort. I was comfortable with Maggie, Ms. Mae. It will take me a while to get comfortable with you. That's not your fault, but you are going to have to deal with it anyway."

Devon nodded.

"Give me some background on you." Joe leaned forward on his desk.

"I came out of the Northeastern Reserve." The younger's voice was hardly lower than Maggie's. "They placed me in the clerical pool. I worked up from there to the IT pool, from there to software development. I was in security software design and testing when the owner of the company retired and liquidated the company. No one wanted my software skills, so I went back to what I did first. I have been doing clerical work ever since."

Joe looked at Devon's blank face. His story had

become all too typical. Work for twenty, forty years building up a company, only to be tossed out to increase someone else's assets. The result - people who should have been making significant contributions to society worked as janitors and file clerks.

"What level are your software skills now?" Joe asked.

"I expect you are using one version or another of software I helped develop. My name won't be there but my code is." Devon smiled at Joe's raised eyebrow. "Let's try something. Pull up your computer. There will be the security window that asks for your name and password. Put White Rabbit in as your user name, upper case W and R, then hookah4321 as the password."

"It says incorrect sign in."

"Click *OK*, and type in the same thing again."

"Still says incorrect sign-in."

"One more time."

"Three incorrect sign-ins will lock up my system and set off alarms at Security." Devon just looked at him, so Joe tried it a third time. Instead of the security window he'd expected, the computer loaded a window he had never seen before.

"Oh boy." Joe said, backing away from the keyboard. "Now what have I done?"

"You followed the White Rabbit into Wonderland. It's a back door I wrote into the last version of the code before they liquidated. Typical – they haven't changed anything major in twenty years. From there, if you are careful, you can access just about anything."

"How do I get out of here?" Joe peered at the screen. It looked nothing like the screens he was used to.

"Use the three finger salute – hit the control, the alt, and the delete keys at the same time."

Joe did what he was told and sighed with relief when his usual screen came up. He looked up at Devon.

"I would ask you to show me more tricks, but I think I've had my limit of excitement for the day. Maggie knew exactly what she was doing when she sent you to me. Now, it's time for you to get to work." He handed Devon a slip of paper. "These are file numbers for cases which have been tagged by someone to prevent further investigation. I would like to know who tagged the files and when. It is very important they don't find out we are looking at this." Devon just nodded and took the paper. He glanced at it briefly and handed it back to Joe.

"To be really safe, I will need a day or two." He got up. "If that is all...?" Joe's new secretary slipped out of the office.

"How did I get so lucky?" Joe got up from his desk and wandered around his office. He stopped in front of the picture of his wife and infant son. He had lived longer without them than he had with them. They were from a different life. Before age had become quite so important.

He had been in corporate security then. Rent-a-cop people called him, but he was good at his job. He handled the physical side of the security, from setting up perimeters to training bodyguards. He had made good calls and ended up working the company president's personal security doing work just as demanding as the Secret Service – work that suited him too.

The asshole who blamed the company for his life going to the dogs decided to get even at the company picnic. That was the first year Joe Jr. was old enough to come. The shooter had aimed at the head table, and Joe had reacted with all his years of training putting himself between the bullets and the company president, pushing his employer to the ground.

Later he was told how the spray of bullets had continued past the intended target to hit a crowd of mothers and children. Even later he'd visited their graves. Then, after he was released from the company hospital where he had been virtually rebuilt with new techniques, he had to learn to live without the people he loved.

He was still learning. Joe adjusted the frame on the wall and ran a finger down one side.

Joe never did understand everything they'd done to him in that hospital, but he knew it had changed him. He quit the company, but took other security work, staying with the only thing he knew.

Long past the time when other security people were pushing desks, Joe still trained, getting stronger and faster. He was young enough to think he was just tougher than the others, but as his colleagues began dying of heart attacks and cancer, he realized it was something more.

There were no records of any of his treatments. He guessed they included some of the more radical gene therapies in vogue at the time. They were never accepted because they didn't give consistent results.

What they did wasn't as important as the result. Joe had outlived everyone he knew. There were only a handful of people in the world who might be older than he was, but not by much. At first he kept his age to himself because he didn't want to deal with the question of why he was still alive, later, because he didn't want to be involved in politics. Now, if it became generally known he was older than two thirds of the Council, there were people who would see him as a serious threat. Anyone with a computer could look it up, but if he kept a low profile, why would they bother?

He told himself that was why he lied to Maggie about his age. He hadn't really been afraid she'd think him a monster if she knew he was more than two hundred years old, but...

Looking for a Ghost

Trey sat in his room and stared at the wall. Two days after the team meeting and he was feeling completely forgotten and inadequate.

Annie had no trouble getting volunteer work at the shelter. Bert brought in her reports, but all they said was the janitor was being treated as a hero for driving off a gang of thieves. Annie was watching him, but didn't expect anything to develop so soon.

Jimmy worked the street checking in with the youth gang he had once run with. He'd quit the gang by having Dan "arrest" him. Now he spun tales of time behind bars and a capricious parole officer. He didn't learn anything new either.

Dan simply practiced his martial arts and meditated. Trey couldn't get his mind to slow down enough for effective meditation. He would listen to his breathing while his brain was pulling in thousands of random thoughts and trying to make sense of them. If he was honest, they weren't all random. There were a lot of thoughts about Red, but he also didn't think he was carrying his weight on the team. Everyone else was out risking their lives while he sat and failed at relaxation.

"I have to get out for a bit," Trey said. Dan just waved at him and went back to the stillness of his meditation. Trey wandered through the halls of the underground. People passed him and gave him a cursory glance. If he was on this side of the doors he must be all right. He found the café where he had shared breakfast with Dan and Red his first morning here. He sat down and a server brought him a coffee.

"I don't have any money," Trey said.

"Don't worry about it," she said, "Not everyone does. It all works out."

Trey sipped his coffee and watched the bustle of activity around him. Everyone seemed to know what was expected of them. Trey had never known what his purpose was. He had vague memories of a father, and was convinced he was just a walking parts reservoir for the man, but something deep inside insisted there was more to his life than that. His inability to make a difference for the Underground didn't help. He might as well have stayed at the Reserve.

"Mind if I join you?" Red said as she slipped into the seat across from him.

"I was hoping you would."

"Why so glum?"

"Everyone knows what they're about." He winced at how much he sounded like he was whining. "I really don't know what I'm doing here."

"So what do you want me to do about it?" Red added milk and sugar to her coffee and stirred it vigorously.

"You are the team leader."

"So you're telling me to lead." She looked at him with a raised brow.

"Well..."

"I don't know enough about you to know how to use you best." Red sipped at her coffee and added more sugar. "I get the feeling you're more than just a brain with feet, but I'm still fitting you in. You don't have connections outside, and as smart as you are, the searches I'm running are beyond your present skills."

"So how is the computer search going?"

"There are too many parameters and it's taking way too long."

"Maybe I can help, I don't know computers as well as you do, but I am good at spotting patterns.

"OK then, finish up your coffee and we'll get started." Red looked at the cup in her hand. "Bleh, I always make it too sweet."

Trey put his cup down and Red led him back to where he had first met the Chief.

Lizzy wasn't there this time. Red showed him the results of her searches so far. The warmth of her looking over his shoulder and occasionally reaching to tap keys distracted him. He set his feelings aside and focused on the words on the screen. Trey lost himself in examining them.

It felt like only minutes later, but when he looked up his neck creaked.

"Ow, how long have we been at this?"

"You've been here all day," Red told him, "I went out and got lunch, but you didn't eat it." She pointed at a plate with a burger and fries sitting at his elbow. "Are you always like this?"

"I don't know," Trey said and took a bite of the burger, "Yech, it's cold." He took another bite and finished the burger. Red whisked the fries away from him.

"I don't think I could stomach watching you eat those. Let's go out for something warm."

"Suits me." Trey pushed himself away from the desk and followed Red out of the room. Lizzy stood in the hallway. She glared at Trey but didn't say anything.

"There are worse things than not knowing your purpose," Red said, "You could know and be trapped by knowing."

Trey wanted to ask her to explain, but his brain, which lined facts and patterns up so neatly, failed to suggest anything to say.

They found a table in the square and Red grabbed a tray.

Trey enjoyed their meal together. Red was close to the impish girl he had first met. She had him in stitches with stories of the team's exploits and disasters. Trey went back to his room feeling better, much better. He lay down on his bunk and let the evening play through his mind. He fell asleep with a smile on his face.

The next days were more of the same. He soaked up information and tried to make sense of it but no pattern jumped out at him. Yet far from being frustrated, Trey was glad because it gave him an excuse to spend more time with Red. He learned to his shock the Chief was Red's father. He had only the faintest memories of his own father to help him make sense of that relationship, but he did know he was envious of the casual way they made it clear how important they were to each other.

He got used to seeing Lizzy and having her glare at him. She always wore long dresses, but gave the impression she could still take him apart, and would enjoy it. So it caught Trey's attention when he saw Lizzy slipping through the crowds in the underground mall wearing an outfit making her look no more than ten. He followed her on impulse. She walked through the halls to a door watched by a man who simply nodded at her as she entered. Trey went to follow, but the man stopped him.

"Sorry kid, you don't have a pass. No pass - no excursions outside."

Trey just nodded and wandered off. He found his way back to the room he shared with Dan.

"I need a pass to go outside."

"You need to ask the Chief," Dan said, "He's the only one who can hand them out."

The next morning Trey asked Red if he could talk to the Chief. She shrugged and took him through several doors to where the Chief was working at a desk.

"I need a pass to go outside," Trey said.

"And why would you need that?" the Chief asked.

"I'm not sure," Trey said, "but we're looking for a ghost, and it is hard to say what might be helpful."

The Chief looked at him for a long time, then looked at Red. She shrugged and nodded. The Chief pulled out a thin piece of plastic.

"Carry this, and you will be able to leave through any of the main doors. Don't abuse it. Vary the doors you use and be careful. You get arrested; we won't be able to help you. Red will see you get some basic top-side training."

Trey put the pass in his pocket and they went back to the piles of data. He had Red look up disappearances in other areas when the Councilor was present and compared them to what he had from their city. For breaks he sat in a tiny room absorbing videos on the risks of moving around outside the Underground and how to avoid them. When he'd finished them, security gave him ID.

"I think there's a pattern developing," he said finally, "It looks like there's people in each region who deal with the Councilor's needs. I'm extrapolating here, but the few witness reports agree on similar vehicles over time. The way the bodies show up suggests the same person is disposing of them. There's an attempt to be different each time, but people naturally fall into patterns. I am much more certain about the disposal than the procuring."

"You need a break," Red said. "Time for supper."

Next day Trey saw Lizzy. Once again she was dressed as a young girl. He followed her through the underground to a different exit. This time the watcher just waved him through. Trey walked out into daylight alone for the first time since Red had found him at the underpass. He just hoped the nanos really were all gone or he would be picked up by the first dogbot that came along.

He had no problems following Lizzy. She hopped and skipped through the people. Most people ignored her, some smiled at her. She meandered her way to a park where she played on the equipment. The other children acted as if she wasn't there. Trey leaned against a tree and watched. Lizzy's play was deliberate while the children were spontaneous. Someone who wasn't watching for the difference would never notice. Lizzy was very good at this.

In the afternoon a man approached the children. Some instinct sent most of them wandering off, but Lizzy stayed playing alone. He struck up a conversation with her, then to Trey's amazement took her hand and led her off. He was even more shocked Lizzy went with him quietly. He followed at a distance, just able to keep the pair in sight. They climbed into a van and drove off. He wasn't going to be able to follow her any more today. He headed back to the door to the underground.

The next day the glare from Lizzy had a different edge to it. Of course she knew he was there, she was always the best at the training games. She'd wanted him to see what he had seen.

He had finally solidified the pattern. Someone was just a little careless, and yet had never been caught. It suggested to Trey this person knew he was under protection. He still couldn't identify who it was.

Unfortunately, the police reports Red managed to access were masterpieces of generalization. The police knew something was wrong and they couldn't do anything about it.

Lizzy came looking for him the next morning wearing shorts and a tee shirt.

"Come," she said and walked away. Trey followed her through the maze of the underground to another door. She led them out into the sun and onto a bus. They were halfway across the city when she left the bus and began skipping down the sidewalk. Trey walked behind trying to act as if he didn't know her. They ended up at another park.

"Wait in the trees," Lizzy ordered as she ran to the swings. Trey walked past the park and around the corner. He found another entrance and made his way back to watch Lizzy engage in her artful play. Once again the other children ignored her, and once again late in the afternoon a man approached her. He was showing her a leash and pointing into the woods. They walked into the woods and ended up where Trey could see them but no one in the park or on the street could.

It was like a switch had been thrown. The leash became a weapon as it wrapped around Lizzy's throat. The man pulled her into him and he groped at her. Trey stepped out to help Lizzy, but before he cleared the bushes the tables had turned. Lizzy twisted the man's hand with more than a child's strength. The man let go of the leash to reach behind him, but it was already too late. Lizzy's foot struck the side of his head, and he sank to his knees. She twisted his arm harder until Trey heard a snap and the man screamed. Lizzy stepped back then carefully kicked the man in the face. He fell back, twitched once then lay still. She checked for a pulse then nodded to herself.

She walked over to Trey.

"Let's go, someone might have heard something." She led him back along the path he had followed into the park. They took a bus which dropped them near a door into the underground. Lizzy only said one thing on the way in.

"Tell no one."

TRAP

Trey had a pattern now, but no way to use it. Without a name they couldn't find the person and question him about selling the children. Likely he wasn't selling them directly to Councilor Molloy, but to the person who disposed of the bodies. They needed a way into the pattern to connect Molloy to the children who were found raped and strangled in corners of the city. Even the police were careful to stay away.

Lizzy continued making him an accessory to her personal hunt. After he had decided not to mention the first outing, it became impossible for him to tell the others. She must have been accessing the Underground's investigations on pedophiles, since she knew exactly where to go and what kind of look she needed.

Trey watched the child-like killer destroy the men who took her to be a helpless innocent. He didn't feel any sympathy for the men, but he was getting concerned she was acting outside of the controls of the team.

"Lizzy, you can't keep doing this," he said once.

"I must," she said. "It is what I am. I am vengeance for the children." She turned away to lead him to yet another death and he almost missed what she said next. "And I need to kill."

The two problems came together for Trey in the middle of the night. He dreamed he was working with Red and she looked at him.

"You're breaking the law, Trey," she said and pulled out a huge gun.

"But it's Lizzy," he started to say.

"Lizzy is just a child," Red said, "So you will die in her place," and her finger tightened on the trigger.

Trey woke with a shout, his heart pounding so hard he was surprised it didn't explode.

"Bad dream?" Dan said from the other bunk.

"Oh yeah," Trey said.

"Don't let it get to you."

Trey stared into the dark of the room and let his heart slow down. As he did an image came into his head. It was a faceless man snatching a girl off the street and giving her to another man in a black car. The only way to make the link was to know the identity of the first man. Or maybe not... Trey had a pretty good idea of where this man hunted his victims. Maybe he would suggest a particular place to hunt to Lizzy next excursion.

When Trey awoke he had a picture of a place and Lizzy dressed in the shorts and shirt that was her hunting outfit. He went to meet Red knowing what he needed to do.

"Red, we need to turn Lizzy loose on our missing link."

She turned to look at him, and he saw an indefinable emotion before she became the team leader.

"Lizzy is hunting solo again."

"Not quite solo."

"I see," she walked over to the computer and typed in a query. "How many?" she asked without turning around.

"Seven, that I know of."

"Seven at least." Her shoulders slumped. "I thought we had dealt with this. What am I going to do with her?"

"Nothing, because you need her. She is the weapon you use to make your political statements. The other teams can do the work, but they have nightmares and feel guilt. Lizzy feels nothing."

"Not nothing," Red said with a sigh. "She enjoys it."

"If I had to say, I would say she was addicted."

"We turned her into a monster."

"She was already a monster," Trey said. "You just used her."

"So how is turning her lose going to help us?"

"We need to get a way into Molloy's organization. We know the janitor provided a girl for him at least once and somehow learned it was for Molloy. If we can cut the regular supply then they will need to go back to the janitor."

"Annie has been watching him, and all he's been doing is cleaning floors."

"I doubt he's reformed. Even if he has, I don't think he would be able to resist Councilor Molloy's people."

"OK, but this is your op. It is just you and Lizzy. I don't want anyone else exposed on this."

"I'll need a car. We can't bring someone back on the bus."

"Take this to the garage and they'll give you training."

Training included more videos, then some time driving around a parking garage. After a brief trip top-side, the security woman declared him cleared to drive.

"Try to avoid damage to the cars," she said as she handed him his license. "It makes the garage people unhappy."

Armed with his new license, Trey went looking for Lizzy.

"We have some work to do," he said without preamble.

"Wait here," she said and walked away. She came back carrying a bag. "Let's go."

Trey explained his plan while they walked to the garage.

"One more thing," he said. "We are back on the grid. Red knows what we are up to."

"She knows about the others?"

"She knows."

Lizzy just nodded and climbed into the car Trey had signed out.

Trey took them to the neighborhood central to the area Molloy's finders found the girls.

"You'll need to troll here," he said. "We need him alive for the moment, but we are going to take him in."

Lizzy shrugged and dropped the long dress on the seat. She pulled the shorts and shirt over a body suit then climbed out of the car. They hunted the area for a week with nothing to show for it.

Trey sat in the car reading a paper when he saw a black car pull into a vacant lot. After a couple of thumps it drove away again. He was bored, so Trey put his paper down and sauntered over to the road. There was no one around as he walked over to the lot. In one corner lay a tangle of white. As Trey got closer he saw the naked body of a young girl, a bit younger than what Lizzy pretended to be. Bruises on her neck showed where she had been strangled. He touched her to check for a pulse. Her eyes opened and she tried to scream through her shattered throat. Trey shouted with surprise and fell over backwards. He looked around, but there was still no one about. He picked her up and wrapped her in his jacket. In a moment they were back at the car and he called Red.

"I need an emergency pickup and medical team."

"Lizzy?"

"No, I will explain later. Hurry."

Lizzy returned just before the team van pulled up.

"Who's she?"

"One of the reasons you're out here." Lizzy just nodded and watched the child until Annie and Bert laid her in the van and drove off.

"I look too old," Lizzy said. Trey just nodded. "Let's

go home. I'll bring different clothes tomorrow."

Jane, as Annie had dubbed the little girl, was in critical condition in the medical unit. Annie watched over her. It didn't surprise Trey. He felt like sitting there and watching too, but he had work to do. He and Lizzy went out again, and somehow she looked younger and more fragile than ever – probably the wig she wore that was closer to Jane's hair in coloring.

A man in a green van roared up beside her and snatched her off the street. Trey followed at a distance. The van didn't travel very fast and it pulled into a vacant lot within a mile and then hung up on a pile of bricks. Lizzy stepped out and kicked the van.

"I hate driving. They just don't make cars for people my size."

When Trey looked in the van the man lay on the floor. There was a red mark the size of Lizzy's shoe on the side of his head. He pulled the unconscious man into his car and put handcuffs on him. Lizzy climbed into the front seat and they sped off. Between the little girl and this man, Trey hoped they had everything they needed.

***

The man they captured didn't want to talk until Lizzy walked into the room and looked at him speculatively, as if she'd discovered a new species of spider.

"Look, I grab the kids matching the guy's instructions. I don't know who he is. I never see him. I message some company I have a package for pickup. Money shows up in my account and the kid disappears from my van."

Back in the briefing room the team went over the possibilities.

"If he isn't the right guy, we're wasting our time," Jimmy said.

"We don't have anything better." Red rubbed her eyes. "If they don't go back to the janitor, we'll do some more trolling. I don't want to put Lizzy at risk. Someone may wonder about a young girl wandering around the city alone. We don't want to be dodging police and social services. Let's give it some time and see what develops."

***

Lizzy lay completely still in the car trunk, focused on the task ahead. The janitor had told them she was supposed to be drugged. Lizzy wasn't going to let anyone drug her, but she could mimic the effect. The car took a careful route through the city, finally slowing after twenty minutes. When the trunk was opened Lizzy could tell from the echoes they were in a closed garage. She felt herself lifted again and carried into a room with much less echo where she was laid on a soft bed. Then came the click of the door closing.

Someone else breathed in the room. Muffled footsteps moved to her head. A hand brushed at her hair, then moved gently, intimately down her body. Lizzy hated to be touched. This was the hardest part of the job. She had to let the target think he was in control. The hand returned to her face, but instead of caressing her, it slapped her viciously.

Lizzy opened her eyes and rolled with the blow.

The Councilor was red faced with fury. He shouted incoherently at her and rained punches and kicks at her. Lizzy could avoid most of them, but some got through. She heard a rib crack and it stabbed her like a knife. The Councilor seemed to wind down suddenly. He started weeping and saying he was sorry. Lizzy was blocked into a corner when he came and knelt in front of her.

"You know it's all your fault," he said, and put his hands around her throat. She wasn't the first person he had strangled. It would only be seconds before she was unconscious, but seconds was all she needed. Her knives leapt into her hands and she buried both of them in his ribs.

He was supposed to die.

Instead he let out a high-pitched scream and fell back from her. Lizzy followed him and stabbed him again and again. Still he wouldn't die. The screaming irritated her, so she cut his throat. He staggered about the room trying to hold the blood inside him and still trying to scream.

The door behind her crashed open and the driver sprang into the room. The sight of a young girl in a bloody dress didn't slow him down. He slashed a kick at her head that would have killed her had it landed, but Lizzy dropped underneath it and cut deep into his femoral artery. Then to be on the safe side she stabbed him a few more times.

An arm came around her throat, cutting off her wind and lifting her feet from the floor. It didn't matter what she hit with her knives; the arm wouldn't loosen. Finally she twisted and stabbed over her head. The broken rib moved and she shrieked with the pain, but the arm let go. She looked into Molloy's mad eyes and stabbed both knives straight through his eyes to his brain. He fell twitching to the bloody floor. Just to be sure, she stabbed the driver through the eyes as well.

Then she sat in the middle of the room and clutched her ribs.

***

Red drove the van, Trey in the passenger seat, Annie and Bert sat in the back. Councilor Molloy was the highest-ranking person they'd ever gone after. It shouldn't have made a difference, but Red was still nervous. They watched the car slip through the garage doors. Red circled the block and parked where they could see the door. It was funny how often people depended completely on their gadgets to make them feel safe, and never looked in the mirror to see if they were being followed. It was why she insisted on radio silence on their missions. You never knew who would hear a stray piece of chatter.

The area they were in wasn't the desperately poor vicinity of the city, but it wasn't the rich suburbs either. They didn't see anyone else around, but that didn't mean they weren't being observed. Red checked her watch yet again.

"She should have called by now." Red looked at her team. "Take a walk past and see if you hear anything."

Trey went with Bert and Annie to stroll along the street.

Annie came back to the van.

"Trey is hearing something odd from the house. He went with Bert to check it out." They waited a couple of minutes, then the garage door opened and a white faced Bert waved them in. Red parked beside the anonymous car and followed Bert through the door. The room was a blood bath. Two bodies lay on the floor and Lizzy sat, obviously hurt in the middle of it. Trey was nowhere to be seen.

"He's gone to check the rest of the house, but it looks like it is empty except for this room." Bert shook his head. "We can't clean this one, not near well enough."

"Then we have to leave it."

"Why not just burn the house down?" Trey asked from the doorway. "There's nothing else here. The places on either side are empty too." Red thought for a moment then nodded.

"We'll have to make it work." She turned back to Lizzy. "Can you walk?" Lizzy nodded and climbed carefully to her feet.

"He wouldn't die," she said. "He just wouldn't die."

"Let's worry about that later," Red said. "We need to get out of here."

Trey and Bert ended up setting the fire, using paints and garbage in the basement. They joined Red, Lizzy and Annie in the van just as smoke started wafting up the stairs. Red waited until they could see the flames before they backed out of the garage and drove off into the city. By nightfall the van was a burned out hulk, and they had stumbled, exhausted, back to their briefing room in the underground.

Aftermath

Trey watched the others pacing outside the operating room. Lizzy's broken rib had punctured a lung. Red and Annie had lifted her onto a gurney and run her in from the garage. Doctors in green scrubs took Lizzie away then denied her friends entry into the inner sanctum. Trey clenched his hands, wishing he could do something useful.

They waited, and while they waited the Chief called them in one by one to debrief them. Most likely any recording had stayed in the house and been destroyed in the fire, but he wanted to know who had entered the room and for how long. He wasn't pleased to learn they had all been there, if only for a few seconds. He put one of the other teams to monitor the net for traffic on the fire, and to learn, if they could, about a possible external feed.

Trey wasn't able to add much to the reports of the rest of the team, but that didn't mean he didn't have some questions of his own. He'd heard Lizzy talk all the way back about how Molloy wasn't human, he wouldn't die. A shudder ran through him. What were they dealing with?

Those pictures they had looked at - the beaten and strangled bodies of children. How could they have looked at those pictures and not seen the perpetrator was violent and dangerous? They had testimony from Jane. Why hadn't they studied her testimony harder?

Trey struggled with his questions. His ability to separate emotion from his thinking failed. Guilt ate at his gut. Now, he had to work through it, get stronger. Though he had been part of his team for only a few months it was the closest thing to a family he had known since the police had separated him from his father. Maybe it was time to start earning his keep. He went to look for Red.

He found her standing outside the medical facility, crying. She turned away to hide her tears.

"It should be raining." Trey said.

"What?" Red looked at him, halfway to angry.

"It is raining outside. It should be raining in here too. Then you wouldn't have to hide your tears."

Red threw herself against him and cried against his shoulder. Trey had no idea what to say so he just held her close and let her cry. It seemed like forever and far too short a time before her sobs became sniffles and she pulled back. He reluctantly let her go.

"It's bad for morale for the team to see their leader cry like a baby."

"It's good for morale for the team to know their leader cares."

"So we'll call it even." Red tried a grin, not quite making it. "If you tell anyone about this I will have to kill you."

"It might be worth it to die in your arms," Trey said. Red gave him a long look. "Oops, did I say that out loud? Pretty corny. I didn't get much practice in intelligent conversation at the Youth Reserves. They pretty much trained us to be industrial cannon fodder."

Red stopped him with a quick kiss on the lips.

"Thank you for being here, and for being you, corny or not." Red took his hand and led him to a bench. "Maybe it is time I told you a bit more about Lizzy." They sat side-by-side while Red kept hold of his hand, playing with his fingers. "All I remember is the Underground, so I had to grow up fast. The Chief is my dad, so it was natural I work in his sector.

"Lizzy is like a sister to me, but no one knows where she comes from. She looks to be eleven or twelve, but she has memories going back at least fifty years. Dad thinks she came out of some illegal experimentation. We found her in a brothel where they had her serving twenty customers a day. As far as we can figure out they had been passing her down from pimp to pimp like some family treasure.

"She was the first person I rescued, about four years ago.

"I've never seen anyone so passive, like an oversized doll. You would pose her and she would stay in that pose. Tell her to say something and she would repeat it back. You can imagine how they were using her. We had a huge fight getting her and the other kids out but we did it and put them into treatment here. For weeks she just sat there, doing only what she was told to. The counselors kept telling her she could make her own decisions, but I think they had given up on her.

"One day an orderly was in too much of a hurry to ask her to move and he just picked her up and moved her. She went berserk. She didn't have any training then so the orderly was just hospitalized. I began training her in martial arts as a way of building her confidence, but it didn't take long for her to learn everything I knew. She needed to see a kata done only once and she could repeat it exactly.

"I brought Dan in to help and soon she had learned everything he knew as well. We tried to teach her the meditation part, and while she can control her body better than anyone I have ever heard of, I don't think she understands the spiritual part of the exercise. After the orderly we gave her very clear instructions she was not to injure any member of the Underground, but she can inflict a lot of pain before she arrives at the threshold of injury as we defined it for her. She has to have the right to defend herself. That's why I warned you to stay clear. She isn't a bad person. She just doesn't play by the same rules as the rest of us."

"Which makes what she said yesterday even more important."

"What do you mean?"

"She kept saying 'He wouldn't die.' If she is as literal as you suggest, then we have to take her comment at face value. It can't be shock making her see things that aren't there, because she isn't wired to see anything but what is actually present.

You saw the body. It had wounds all over it. I'm not sure, but I would think any one of those wounds would be enough to kill."

"So what are you suggesting?"

"I think it is too bad we burned the house so quickly. The doctors might have been interested in what Molloy's body had to tell us."

Red shook her head.

"Another thing I did wrong."

"It isn't a total loss. We still have the blood on her dress."

Red smacked her head and dashed back into the medical center. Trey followed a few steps behind. Red stood at the security counter talking rapidly into the phone. He waited for her to finish.

"We caught them in time. Just." She waved him on. "She's awake, and wants to talk to me. You're coming too. Don't worry, I'll protect you." They ran up the stairs to the recovery room. Red stopped briefly to give the news to the others and tell them to write up their reports in as much detail as they could.

The recovery room was dim and hushed. Electronics stood pushed against the wall. Lizzy lay in the bed with the sheets pulled up to her chin. She saw Trey and frowned. Red went over to the bed and crouched down.

"You gave me a scare, girl. You're not supposed to get beat up like this. It is back to the training room for you."

"Sorry, Red." Lizzy's whisper sounded painful.

"I'm joking, girl. You did great. I need to hear what happened if you are ready to talk."

"Why him?"

"He convinced me how important it was to hear your report."

"Water."

Red held the glass while Lizzy took a sip.

"Driver carried me in. Left me on the bed. I could hear breathing. He touched me." Lizzy shuddered at the memory. "Then he hit me." She pointed at her face. "He kept hitting me and kicking me. He wasn't a good fighter, but strong. I tried to get close enough to use the knives. He strangled me, and I stabbed him in the heart and in the liver. I didn't miss. He just screamed and fell back. I stabbed him in both lungs, the kidneys, the spleen. He wouldn't die. I cut his throat to stop him screaming.

"That's when the driver came in. He tried a strong kick. I cut his femoral artery. I stabbed his heart, lungs and spleen. The first one came up behind me and put a chokehold on me. I stabbed him more...I don't know where...sorry. Then I stabbed his face, hitting his eye. He loosened the hold and I stabbed his brain through each eye. He died. Then I stabbed the driver through each eye, he was dead too."

Trey thought for a moment.

"Lizzy, may I ask a couple of questions?" Lizzy looked at him for a long moment.

"Ask."

"What else was different about him?"

"His face was red, but it was the wrong red. His voice was wrong. He said, 'know it is all your fault.' He brought me there. It was not my fault. He fought badly. He was too strong."

"Thank you, Lizzy. May I come back later? I will have something for you to listen to."

"With Red." Lizzy looked stubbornly at Red.

Red shrugged.

"Fine. See you later." Trey waved and left the two in the room. The waiting area was empty, so Trey walked back to the briefing room and sat at one of the computer terminals. The program he was looking for wasn't one of the ones they used, so it took him a while to find it. After an hour or two of experimenting he had a result he hoped was close enough. He downloaded it to a player and went looking for Red. He found her where he thought she would be, still at Lizzy's side.

"Hello, Lizzy. Are you ready to listen?"

"Ready."

Trey pushed the play button.

"You know it is all your fault." The voice was odd. Lizzy's eyes widened, and she looked around.

"Does it sound like him?" Trey switched off the player.

"Like, but not the same," Lizzy said. "He sounded higher, not as breathy."

"Thanks, Lizzy," he said. "That's a big help."

"Explain, please?"

"I can't be certain, but his blood will tell us more. I think Councilor Molloy was artificial. That's why he wouldn't die when you stabbed him, because what are vital organs for a person aren't for a machine."

"He wanted... what a machine doesn't want."

"Maybe his brain was still human. It would explain why he died when you stabbed through his eyes."

"I stab through eyes now."

"Probably a good idea."

"Trey," Lizzy said. "Thank you for believing me." She turned to Red. "I will sleep now." Red nodded and stood up.

"OK, girl. Sleep well."

When the door closed behind them Red leaned against Trey. He hugged her close.

"I could get used to this," he whispered.

"Mmmmph," she said into his chest.

They stood there a long while until Red finally stepped back and Trey forced his arms to let her go. They stood there looking at each other.

"The Underground comes first, Trey," she said apologetically. "I can't let myself get distracted. I got careless, and almost got Lizzy killed. I can't afford to let it happen again."

"I understand, Red. I do, but it doesn't mean we can't take time to prepare ourselves for after."

"For after what?"

"For after we win."

Red laughed and Trey stepped up and gave her a quick kiss on the lips.

"If we don't think about after, then we waste everything we have done." He held her close.

Red touched her lips, and smiled.

"You do have a point. Let's get to work on the winning part." She grabbed his hand and tugged him after her.

***

Lizzy rolled her head back toward the ceiling and tried to think about what she had seen through the translucent glass on the door, but the tears pouring out her eyes prevented all thought.

DISCOVERIES

A subdued team met in the briefing room. Red walked in and looked around at them. She tossed a file on a side table.

"I haven't seen so many long faces since I visited the donkeys at the petting zoo." She sighed dramatically. "Lizzy will be fine, and we have some good information from the raid. So, let's look at what we'll do differently next time."

"We need to do more scouting before we go out," Dan said. "We were overconfident."

"We can't just depend on Lizzy to do all the dirty work for us," Jimmy banged on the table. "We need to have backup teams and be prepared to take people out ourselves. There is no way she should have had to kill two people. The driver should have been neutralized before he went back in."

"We were upset and got sloppy." Trey rolled his head to relax his tight shoulders. "We should have brought samples from the house back, maybe even Molloy's body. We can't assume we know what we are dealing with. We know there's some strange stuff out there. We have Lizzy. What might they have? Has anyone checked to see the news reports on the fire? There aren't any. As far as the rest of the world is concerned there never was a fire. Councilor Molloy isn't mentioned in the news either. It will be interesting to see how they spin his death. We can send our evidence as usual, but I don't think it will get any play. I think the killing of perverts in the government has turned out to be a waste of time and resources." Trey wound down as he saw how the others looked at him. He saw Red trying not to smile. She winked at him.

"What do you mean by that?" Jimmy half stood up to glare at Trey.

"I put pieces of puzzles together, extrapolate possibilities and figure out where to look for the evidence to fill in the gaps. It all tells me we're going the wrong direction.

"So now you tell us what to think? Next thing you'll be wanting to be team lead --"

"I looked at his file from school." Red interrupted Jimmy. "Even with him getting himself into more trouble than you did in class, his scores are off the charts. Someone has been going through his file year after year and lowering Trey's scores so he just looks brilliant instead of what he is."

"And what is he?" Jimmy sat down and slumped in his chair.

"I don't know, but I intend to find out." Red answered. "So I'm cutting him loose and letting him find his own limits. Annie and Bert, you'll help Trey find whatever he needs. No more excursions without the express permission of the Chief or me. Jimmy, you and Dan and I will rework our strategy so we don't leave someone on their own again."

"I still don't like this," Jimmy said.

"Jimmy, I've been with you and Dan all morning. Right?" Trey said.

"Yeah."

"So I couldn't know what is in the file Red brought in and laid on the table in the corner. I can tell you with a fair degree of certainty what it is. I expect it is preliminary results from the blood on Lizzy's dress. The results will say there is two persons' blood on the dress, and one of them is Lizzy's."

"But she killed two people. Their blood was all over the place," Annie said. "There would have to be three different blood matches."

"Assuming what was in Molloy was blood. It looked like blood, but I think it was an artificial fluid. Molloy wasn't flesh and blood the way we are. I suspect though he was always a bit warped and he became progressively less sane over time. I have no idea how living in an artificial construct would affect the psyche. Humans are not just brains in a body. I played a computer simulated voice for Lizzy and she agreed it sounded like Molloy."

Red went over to the file, picked it up and dropped it in front of Jimmy.

"Check it out."

He flipped the file open and started reading. He went white, then red and pushed it away from him. Bert grabbed it and read for himself then passed it to Annie. It went all around the table until it got to Trey.

He flipped through it and saw he had been correct in just about every particular. Trey looked up and saw Jimmy glaring at him. He wished it hadn't been Jimmy again. It was like being back at school, always trying to hide what he was.

"Artificial people, brains in robots? What are we talking about here?" Annie's eyes were wide. Bert put his hand over hers.

"We knew the world was getting stranger..." He trailed off and shrugged.

"A brain in a new body would need to relearn everything," Dan shook his head. "I know I wouldn't want to do it."

Red put her hand on Trey's shoulder.

"Games are done, my dears. Time for work. You know what to do."

No, not like school. I don't need to hide here. If they could accept Lizzy, they could accept him. Though, seeing Jimmy's black look, it might be harder for some.

Red took Jimmy and Dan out of the room with her. Annie and Bert looked at Trey.

"Well Trey, you're the boss. Tell us where to start." Annie gave him a level stare.

"I need to know everything I can about the Underground. I seemed to have missed the usual sightseeing tour, so assume I know absolutely nothing. Anything you are uncomfortable sharing, check it out with Red or the Chief. Computer files or the printed word is faster for the details, but I would like an overview right now if you can. I would also like details on the previous criminals the Underground has eliminated, including any fallout after their execution."

"I'll gather the old files, Annie. You always do the history class better." Annie stuck her tongue out at Bert, but swiveled back to Trey.

"You look to be about...seventeen? About the same age as our fearless leader. Be careful, she's not as tough as she looks." She tilted her head and looked at him. "But you might be good for her. Just be careful of the jealous type."

"You mean Jimmy?"

"Poor Jimmy, he's had a crush on her since she rescued him. She's just not right for him, but he hasn't found the one who is yet.

"But to business. Pay attention. This will be on the test. The Underground started as most of these movements do, as widely spread and poorly organized cells of discontent. Young people who were feeling more and more left out of life, middlers who saw their working life stretch interminably into the future. Did you know the average working life use to be about 40 years, after which you could enjoy a retirement of maybe fifteen years before your health collapsed and you were warehoused until you died?

"As medical research pushed back the threshold of the body's collapse, the age for retirement was pushed back as well because you needed more money to pay for the longer life after retirement. Some people who were on the borderline of being able to afford retirement kept working after they reached the age of eighty to build up their pension income. Still, not everyone was able or willing to support their own old age, so pension requirements became the largest single deduction from wages, hitting fifty percent in the last twenty years. They're still going up because there aren't enough new workers entering the system. So they created the Youth Reserves.

"Most folks think they are for the children who don't have adequate family support, but in fact they're carefully managed to increase the birth rate in certain sectors of the population. The inmates are drugged to reduce the sex drive while they are there, given no contact or real education about the sex drive and procreation. When they are sent out into the world the first thing they do is have huge uncontrollable families who then become the next generation of children in the Youth Reserves.

"In the wealthy there is an obligation to replace yourself, but no more. Too many children of wealth will split the power base. Your name suggests your father was deliberately breaking that unwritten rule. The enclaves for the wealthy families are as isolated as the Youth Reserves, but for different reasons. They don't want the next generation of rulers to be corrupted by contact with the rest of humanity. As bad as they are, the Youth Reserves are better off than the completely destitute who populate most of the cities. If the poor have jobs, they will never earn enough to retire, and they probably won't live that long anyway. They scrape by getting so caught up in the struggle for survival it never occurs to them life could be better.

"From these three groups the discontent grew

and the cells began bumping into each other. A group of morally outraged rich would encounter some labor atrocity and try to push for reform. Each time they were rebuffed some gave up and put blinkers on, but a few continued to struggle for justice. Those few met a group of destitute poor in the city who knew all the abandoned places to hide. Wealth and knowledge grew to include a possibility for creating a parallel society where some fairness is possible. Word spread through rumor and other discontents joined."

"So they started the Underground." Trey nodded.

Annie's summary matched his assessment of the power structures back at the Reserve.

"The Underground became structured the way you see it now about eighty years ago; for most of its history it existed as a separate, alternative society. In the last twenty years, as the outside society became more repressive we have become more active in recruiting. Ten years ago it became apparent it was no longer enough to provide shelter for people society was abusing, but we needed to actively work to change the society we were hiding from. We don't have the room to just hide anymore.

"We also don't have the resources to take on the government head on, even if we wanted to. So it was decided to try a strategy of attrition. We would eliminate the worst offenders against the young, and support those who respected the humanity of all ages.

"Unfortunately it's a long slow process, and

some of the younger people want their new society now. The biggest advantage the Geris have is they can afford to wait".

Trey waited while the information percolated through his consciousness. He wasn't really sure how he did what he did, but he knew how to make it work. He got up.

"Let's go for a walk," he said. They left a note for Bert and went out into the tunnels.

"How do you fit into the picture?" he asked Annie.

"Bert brought me in. Bert's family wasn't rich, but they were proud none of their family was out of the Youth Reserves. I came out of the Southwestern Reserve as horny as any rabbit and just as smart. Bert treated me properly, which frustrated me to no end. As I got used to not having the drugs in my system I learned some self-control. Bert's mom told me how things worked and I got really angry at how I had been set up.

"We struggled for a bit, but decided we were meant for each other anyway. We were going to get married, but we couldn't come up with the extra dollars for the family pension payment. It was more than both of us were making at the time. A friend of Bert's told him about the Underground. He checked it out then brought me here. We've been married about a year. No extra fees, no extra pension. We aren't rich, but we aren't poor either. Up there, they want people so busy padding their own nest they don't see they are stealing from their neighbor's nest. The rich, they are stealing from everybody."

"Time to go back," Trey said. They turned and walked back. Bert was waiting for them. He raised an eyebrow, but some unseen signal from Annie made him relax.

"Here's a start on those files. I'll have more tomorrow. I had to run some past the Chief."

"Why not just set me up on the network?"

"All these files are hard copy only," Bert said. "You can't hack into paper."

"Thanks, Bert. I am going to be a while, and I need some quiet."

"Ooh, Bert, let's go and make noise somewhere else." Annie winked at Trey. The files absorbed his attention and he didn't notice them leave.

MORE TROUBLE

Trey pored through the files soaking in information like a sponge. They didn't take long to read, but he kept changing their positions to reflect new correlations. Data swam in his head and he barely noticed when Red brought him food. He ate without thinking. When he couldn't keep his eyes open any longer he slept. When he woke there were new files on the table, and he started the process again.

Trey didn't know what he was looking for, but the unease grew in his gut. There was something wrong. He needed to find it. Another day passed mechanically. The pile of new information dissolved under his scrutiny, but the problem still didn't become clear.

"Enough for now," Red said as she shook his shoulder. "A girl can take being ignored for only so long."

"Huh?" Trey looked at her and tried to focus his eyes.

"That's the most intelligent thing you've said all day."

"Sorry, Red." Trey pushed away from the table. He staggered when he tried to stand up. Red caught him and put a strong arm around his waist. Trey rested his arm around her shoulders and let the warmth of her body soak into him. When she pulled him out of the room he didn't protest. There was no way he was going to break the precious contact. They walked in silence through the deserted halls. She brought him to the café in the mall where they sat with entwined fingers and drank their coffee. Red put too much sugar in hers again. This time Trey poured coffee from his cup to make it less sweet.

"I thought we're supposed to be working our asses off." Jimmy threw himself into the seat next to them. Trey started to pull his hand back, but Red's fingers tightened on his so he left his hand where it was.

Jimmy scowled. "Here I was hoping genius here would have some new info for us, and all he's doing is trying to make time with his group leader."

Red sighed and sat back. Trey reluctantly let her hand slip from his.

"Jimmy, what I do on my own time is no business of yours." Red's team leader voice had returned.

"That's not what you told me before." He looked on the verge of violence, or tears.

"You're right." She sighed and looked at the table then met Jimmy's eyes. "I should have been honest with you. I like you, Jimmy, but not the way you want me to. "

Jimmy stared at her for a long moment, then he stood up and fled from the table. Red looked at where Jimmy had disappeared into the crowd.

"I failed him, Trey," she said. "I didn't have the courage to just tell him 'no'. So I fell back on being his team leader, I couldn't be his girlfriend. If I had been honest with him from the start, this would never have happened."

"Or maybe it would have," Trey said. "He doesn't seem to be the kind to take *'no'* easily."

"But there is still the part about being a team leader," Red said. "I can't be your team leader and be in love with you too. I need to talk to Dad about this." She got up from the table and gently kissed Trey's forehead. "It's the best coffee I've ever had."

Trey watched her disappear into the swirl of people contemplating the crowds for a long time. seeing the patterns in their movements emerge. Behind the patterns were the design choices. That booth could be moved over a little to make the flow easier and give the people shopping at it more space to stand.

Anything to avoid thinking about Red walking away from the table, and leaving him alone. Love didn't feel anything like he thought it should.

He finally walked back to the room with the table and the files and dove into the data again.

Annie came in with some food and Trey told her he needed still more information. A little while later another box of files appeared. Finally, he stopped trying to force the solution. He just watched and waited to see what emerged. There was a pattern in the way some of the pedophiles they had executed had been replaced. Some of them, while abusers, had been middle of the road politically. Their replacements were hard liners against youth rights. Worse, they were in a position to have a direct effect on justice for youth, children and families.

He looked deeper into those cases. It looked more and more like someone wanted particular people killed, and was using the Underground to do the dirty work. Trey couldn't find any manufactured evidence, but the break in each case was a slip of the tongue by an informant. None of them involved the usual background search for the perpetrator; just the investigation to show the tip was a good one. The executions rising from the more detailed investigations were spread over the entire political spectrum; their replacements leaned in no specific direction.

It was all too easy. In Councilor Molloy's case they should never have known the connection between him and the murdered girls. The janitor at the shelter shouldn't have known he was procuring for the councilor, but he had. Someone had told him because they wanted the Underground to know. Yet Molloy hadn't been replaced. He was still showing up on the vids, more now than ever. The Council, or someone close to them worked hard to keep Molloy alive in the eyes of the public. After some research, Trey found it hard to imagine a more hard line position against youth.

Molloy's death was different reason for other reasons too. The thing Lizzy had killed was artificial. Maybe that was part of it.

Trey went back to the other deaths and tried to

make sense of them. He thought of the booth being moved to ease traffic. These people had been in the way. He wasn't sure of what.

He went back to the files and this time laid out the positions the abusers had held. What advantage would it confer the nameless force to hold power over those jobs? They ranged from a director of social services to an enforcement branch dealing with disruptive families, to a licensing bureau overseeing contracts. They all involved the interface of government and the Youngers. He pulled up information to see what kind of actions these new people had taken. Each policy change shifted resources away from the Youngers and their families.

It made sense only if they wanted resentment to boil over into open conflict. The person behind this knew about the existence of the Underground and could be trying to force it into the open. Conflict would only strengthen the government's position, maybe even lead to the loss of even more rights for the young. His unease transformed into dread. The changes were escalating.

Perhaps Molloy didn't move fast enough. Being over two hundred might make someone overly cautious. With a virtual Molloy being manipulated by someone behind the scenes, the plan could go ahead sooner.

Too soon.

Time for him to talk to Red. He went looking for her, but the Underground was deserted. Must be late at night. Trey had no idea where her room was since she usually just showed up whenever he needed her.

Trey went back to his room and woke Dan.

"I need to talk to Red."

"Now?" Dan sat up.

"Now."

"This had better be important."

"It is."

"It can't wait until morning?"

Trey paused and thought for a moment. The urgency pushed at him.

"I don't think so."

"Well, let it be on your head then." Dan swung himself out of bed and dressed quickly. "Follow me."

He led Trey through the halls to a door then knocked with a complicated rhythm. When there was no response he knocked again. Trey heard some muffled cursing through the door before it was flung open.

"This had better be important." Red saw Trey standing with Dan and frowned slightly.

"This was his idea," Dan said, "Goodnight kids." He ambled away down the hall.

"Trey --"

"I need to talk to my team leader." Trey watched the change as Red adjusted her thinking. She stood up straighter and her eyes focused like lasers on him.

"Meet me at the office in ten." She closed the door.

At the office Trey paced back and forth until Red arrived.

"Well, make it good." She slouched in a chair.

Trey filled her in on the process of his work. Her

fingers tapped impatiently. But when he started talking about the manipulation of the Underground by some outside force, she stood up and walked around the office. He didn't think he had ever seen her so upset. When he finished she took his hand.

"You need to talk to Dad." She dragged him through the tunnels turning back and forth. She stopped at a blank door. "Don't tell anyone about this, not even the team members." She put her hand on a slightly darker smudge on the door and a thin line of light outlined it. The door swung open and she dragged him in. He had barely cleared the door when it slammed shut. "Don't waste time. It opens for only five seconds. If you try to jam it every alarm in the place will go off." She struck out again through the dimly lit corridor.

Trey reflected he seemed to be following Red around a lot. At least the view was nice. She rounded a corner and stopped. Trey took the opportunity to bump into her. She gave him a distracted peck and put a finger up against her lips. Trey could just hear some muffled voices on the other side of the wall. After a few minutes Red shook her head and leaned against Trey. He dutifully put his arm around her. It was somehow very comforting to just stand there with her head on his chest. Her breathing evened and slowed, the fog of exhaustion settled into his mind.

They waited about twenty minutes before the voices faded and a section of the wall swung open. Red made no move to step away from Trey, so he just looked up.

"Hello, Chief." He shook Red's shoulder gently. "Your Dad's here."

"S'alright, Hi Dad." She reluctantly stepped back but retained Trey's hand.

The Chief looked at the two of them and shook his head.

"You didn't bring him here so I could watch you snuggling."

"Trey has stuff to tell you."

The Chief waved them through the wall into a room painted a stark white and rolled over to a desk in the corner. Screens on the wall were blank. The table was a dark wood surrounded by chairs begging to be sat in. So Trey sat, then had to test the swivel. His knees banged into Red's and she giggled. They stared at each other until the Chief cleared his throat.

"You are going to tell me...stuff?"

"Right, Chief, stuff." Trey took a deep breath and shook his head. Red snored charmingly in her chair, slowly circling.

"Son, when was the last time you slept?"

"Well, we brought in Lizzy after making a hash of our assignment. Then, we waited up most of the night while she was in surgery. After considering the blood, we got them to check the dress. We figured he was artificial and the blood confirmed it. I made a computer voice and it sounded like him, so he must be fake, but maybe his brain was real, and that's why he died. After a brief meeting, Annie gave me a quick history of the resistance and we took a walk. Bert brought me some files so I looked at them. Then more files. Red forced me to take a break, then more files. I think I slept yesterday, or maybe it was the day before."

"I got most of this in Red's report on the action, and the stuff?"

"Stuff?"

"The stuff you are going to tell me."

"Someone is manipulating the Underground to kill for them. They want to start a war. It's going to be soon. I can't tell you when." He poured out all his conclusions yet again fighting through the mud in his brain.

"By soon, do you mean in days, weeks, months?" The Chief shook Trey gently. "To people who are two hundred years old, soon might be next year."

"Killing Molloy was the last piece. It started the end game. Not a year, soon."

Trey put his head on the table and tried to reach his hand toward Red. The Chief gently stopped Red's circles and put her hand on Trey's. They linked fingers and the last thing Trey heard was the Chief tapping away at the computer.

UNSETTLING PATTERNS

Joe was working at his desk when Devon knocked and brought coffee in.

"I hope I'm right and you drink it black," he said handing a steaming cup to Joe. He took a lighter colored cup for himself.

"Making coffee isn't in the job description."

"No, but it's a good excuse for a break. I find I need to step back and let my subconscious work. It works better with caffeine."

Joe just raised his cup to Devon in salute. They finished their coffee in companionable silence. Joe was more impressed with this Younger every time he met him. When he put the empty cup down on the desk, Devon set his aside.

"What do you know about Councilor Molloy?" Devon asked.

"He is one of the five Eldest, had some unspecified health problems and pretty much retired from the public eye. He's still active in the Council as Chair."

"Someone very high in his office put the tags on those files." Devon looked up briefly.

Joe stared at his assistant.

"Yeah, that's pretty much what I thought too." Devon twisted his fingers together. The first sign of nerves Joe had seen in him. "So I did some other checking. Someone very clever has been tiptoeing through the Elder Justice files. I found a total of twelve tagged files; the six you already have, two you haven't found yet, and four that are closed. All the dead were killed in the same manner."

"By stabs to the heart and liver, with extremely sharp knives left in the wounds until the victim was dead and blood would have stopped flowing.."

Devon shuddered slightly.

Breathe, the kid just started here. "The M.O. shows up in a number of other cases."

"All of the victims were linked to crimes against children. Most of the victims were also in positions of some trust." Devon's voice took on an edge of anger.

"Interesting, many of the ones with least real authority were black file cases. They were bureaucrats."

Joe leaned back and stared up at the ceiling.

"So what do you want me to do with this information?" Devon asked.

"Nothing, for now. I will have to find a way to see Councilor Molloy."

Devon looked impressed. He took the coffee cups and left Joe to find a way to meet with the most powerful man in the country.

Joe sat at his desk for a long time then decided it was time to call in a favor. He picked up his phone and hit the encrypt button. Even as he did he thought about Devon out in the front office, and wondered who had programmed the phone, and what back doors there were through its security. He shrugged. Nothing he could do about it now.

"Deputy Chancellor Mulholland. It's Joe, the Methuselah. I am hoping you can do something for me. I need to meet with a member of the Council. I could use your help in gaining an introduction." He hung up the phone and sat back. There was nothing to do now but wait for the Chancellor to return his call.

He tried to distract himself with other work. The complaints had been piling up while he worried at the problems the killings presented. Most were things he could deal with over the phone. Some were outside of his jurisdiction. Some complaints about unfair changes in contract licensing should be sent to the head of the department. The name of the woman heading that department rang a bell.

A cold hand clutched his heart. She was one of the replacements for a black file victim. He looked through the other complaints. Two more were from departments now headed by people replacing black file victims.

Joe ran a search on complaints and wasn't surprised to learn the volume had increased dramatically, most directed at twelve specific departments. Someone had taken advantage of the killings to put hard-liners in place. He couldn't imagine the group behind the killings being in position to control the replacements. A deep game was being played here, and he didn't like the looks of it.

The phone rang. A nondescript male voice informed him D.C. Mulholland was very sorry, but he wouldn't be able to help. Both he and the Chancellor were tied up in negotiations with the delegation from Japan. Joe loathed the computer callers, but the message was too important to hang up.

He buzzed Devon.

"Where are the negotiations with the Japanese delegation taking place?"

"Ahh, they are currently eating lunch at a steak house on the west side famous for its Kobe beef. I'm afraid the Council is in for an embarrassment. The restaurant hasn't used Kobe beef in the past five years."

"Well if they are already going to be embarrassed, I probably will be a welcome distraction. Please call up a car for me." Joe picked up his cane and stumped out to the elevator. *Just like old times. Whoopee.*

The car met him at the door and whisked him off to the famous steak house. It took longer and longer stares for him to get through the layers of security. He actually had to show his I.D. at the door to the restaurant. He walked in after removing the battery to his charge cane and leaving it with the guards at the door. He didn't bother installing the backup in his jacket pocket. If things got that bad, his cane wasn't going to save him.

He saw the Japanese first. They were bowing at the chefs from the restaurant. As he watched, a Younger aide came up and muttered to him.

"They don't do that so much anymore, but they know it confuses us." Joe glanced at the aide and saw he was one of the many Youngers forming Mulholland's team. "The Chairman isn't here. Not in person. The Japanese are upset they don't get to meet one of our Eldest face to face. He was very apologetic but other concerns have him trapped, and he hoped they would get on well with the Deputy Chancellor."

Oh well, at least I'll get to eat some fake Kobe beef.

***

Two days later Joe watched Councilor Molloy on a large screen addressing some recipients of Life Service Awards. The day after, Councilor Molloy took part in a conference call on the issue of family ghettoes. A few days later he again appeared larger than life. Joe gave up and returned to his cave of an office.

"What happened?" he asked Devon during their morning coffee ritual. "Why is he suddenly all over the place on TV when he hasn't shown his face in public in ten years?"

"I think the videos are computer generations," Devon said. "I've been running algorithms on his speeches. His pronunciation and word usage is too consistent. The multiple appearances may be to prove he is still active and alive."

"So you are saying he might be dead?" Joe asked.

"I don't have enough information to say," Devon replied. "But I am sure the videos are not him."

"Wonderful," Joe said. "I won't be able to see his face when I hint about the black files."

The coffee was done and Devon took the cups back into the front office. Joe was stymied. Everywhere he turned his investigation was blocked. He was ordered to stay away from Trey. Mulholland was out of bounds as well. The black files were still tagged. Even all the other files were out of reach in Roberta's office. Now, Councilor Molloy was either dead or out of commission. He wasn't sure how things could get worse.

Devon came back into the office with a mini drive.

"This was left on my desk while we were having coffee. I checked it on my computer for possible software bombs or other attacks, but it appears to be just files. You can access it safely."

"Do you know what's on it?" asked Joe.

"I checked for security issues. I didn't look at the content."

"OK, let's have a look." Joe waved the assistant around to his side of the desk. He plugged the drive into his computer and pulled up the files. There were pictures and text. They purported to prove Councilor Molloy was a child molester and a killer. They also claimed he had been executed by the Child Crimes Killer and closed with an address in one of the poorer city neighborhoods.

"You didn't see this." Joe's heart pounded painfully. "Not until I get some outside verification. If you can check the allegations without setting off alarms do it. I also need whatever you can get on that address between now and when I arrive there."

Joe took his cane and almost ran out of the office.

"I'll call you a car."

Joe just waved as the door closed behind him.

The car took him to the address where the house had burned to a hulk. The houses on either side showed some damage as well. He got as close as he could safely, and contemplated his next step. While he stood there an older woman came up to him in a dressing gown. It was faded to grey and matched the no-longer fuzzy slippers. The only concession she made to the late fall weather was the kerchief around her hair.

"You looking for the young punks what set that fire?"

"I am."

"Just because we live in a poor neighborhood, they think they can take their sweet time responding. We might have lost a whole lot more if the Old Man hadn't got some firefighters to put their hoses on them two side houses."

"If you will excuse me." Joe pulled out his cell. "Devon, please check on response time to a fire in this neighborhood..." He turned to the woman. "What day did you say it was?"

"Well, let me see I was watching that new game show, and my Old Man hadn't come home from what he calls work yet. I had chicken in the oven, my man's favorite. So it would be Thursday past, about 7:30."

"Did you get that? Thanks, call me back."

"You were telling me about the young punks."

"The usual car pulled into the garage. Nice car, but not stand out if you know what I mean. But my Old Man always drooled over that car. He was sure it was modified to the nines. It pulls in, garage door closes, same old same old, if you know what I mean. Then the van pulls up over there" She pointed across the street. "I was peeved because they were blocking my view. They sit there for maybe half an hour. Then some young punks get out and wander oh so casually by the house.

"Next thing I know one of them has broken in and opened the garage door. The van pulls into the garage, but they leave the door open. Punks are all over the place. They even check the places next door. Next thing I know they carry some kid covered with blood into the van. Do they take off? No, they sit there until even I can see the smoke and flames. Then they leave, driving real casual like. I called the fire department, but you know how long they take to arrive."

"We didn't find a car in the garage." Joe looked at the woman. "Maybe we can make a deal. You let my people look at the car, and I will forget it ever existed."

"In the back, you be careful though. My Old Man is so hot for that thing, I think he would rather sleep with it than me."

"Devon," he said into the phone. "I need our best forensics team here immediately. I want them to go over the house with a fine-tooth comb. I will also need them to look at a car."

The team arrived within the hour and, looking like alien invaders in their white suits and masks, crawled all over the burned out house. A couple of the team followed the neighbor woman to check out the car in the back of her house. Joe stood on the sidewalk and watched. He talked to a couple of other bystanders but only learned the house was usually deserted. Once a month or so the car would go into the garage, leave a few minutes later and then return anywhere up to an hour later. It would leave hours later or even the next day. As the crowd got cold and nothing more interesting happened they went back into their homes.

"Hey mister, you want, I can tell you who used that crib." Joe looked at the speaker. She looked to be twelve at the most. "It'll cost you twenty."

"Twenty's a lot of money, but if you really know who used the house, it could be worth a lot more." Joe looked at the girl again. "I could give you twenty right now and you tell me, or you tell me and I pay you what I think it's worth."

"You could figure it ain't worth nothing, and I'm out. You pay me ten for talking to you. Then I'll show you."

Joe pulled a ten out of his pocket.

"That's fair." She made the money disappear then looked around.

"Follow me."

Joe walked after the girl. She led him around to the back of the house.

"This is the only room he ever used. Weird old fart. Everything else is dust. Tommy dared me to look through the window one time he was here." Her voice hitched for a second. "I took a picture of him. Tommy wanted to blackmail the geezer, but guys like him, you don't blackmail. You just die." She handed him a cell phone and punched a few buttons. A picture of Councilor Molloy came up. He was strangling a young girl. Joe forwarded the photo to Devon.

Joe pulled out some cash and gave it to her along with her phone.

"One more thing. Can you give me your number so I can call you if I need more information?" The girl thought for a minute, then looked at the wad of cash in her hand.

"Sure" She rattled off a number then vanished. He picked his way back to the street and called Devon.

"I want everything you can find on this number, especially file transfers. Be on the lookout for activity on this site. My being here is going to upset whoever is pulling strings. Maybe they'll reveal themselves to slap me down."

"I will call you back in a few minutes."

"We have finished our preliminary scan." The forensics specialist stood patiently beside Joe. She had obviously waited for him to finish his call.

"Any findings?"

"The house was not only burned but cleaned

out. The car itself is a ghost. There's no record of registration or ownership. We ran the serial number and discovered it was fake. There were two blue hairs in the trunk." She held up an evidence bag. "From the length I am guessing female. I will have them tested at the lab, but it is unlikely they will show up in any database. We found some blonde hairs, probably from a wig. We left the car where it was as you instructed. Nothing else to find there." The specialist pointed toward the house.

"There was something else in the house. I've never seen anything like it. The fire melted the thing down past the point where it could be easily removed. Early results are consistent with past experiments with artificial body parts."

"Thanks," Joe said. "Send any further reports to my office."

The tech smiled and went back to her team.

Joe walked back to his car. "My office, please." The driver pulled out smoothly. Joe thought hard all the way back. Molloy was abusing and killing children. The picture from the phone might have put the resistance on to him. Legwork would have done the rest. But if Molloy had gone well past the treatments that were the privilege of the elite it didn't save him. The question remained, who was pretending to be Molloy now?

INFORMATION

Trey woke to the smell of coffee and the warmth of a hand in his. He looked at Red sleeping quietly, somehow curled up in the chair and still holding his hand.

"She's quite something." The Chief sat in the corner of the room sipping his coffee. "I've been wondering when she would fall for something more than her rebellion. You take care of her, Trey, but just keep in mind she is her own person."

"I will, sir." Trey admired Red again, She looked so sweet sleeping, though he didn't think she'd appreciate him telling her that. "Have you been here all night?"

"She may be her own woman, but I am still her father."

"Understood."

"Coffee?" The Chief waved a cup in Trey's direction.

"Better make it two, she's waking up." Red stretched luxuriously and Trey released her hand. Suddenly her eyes snapped open. She took in Trey and her father and squealed.

"I must look a mess!" She ran through the door.

Trey sighed. "I'll take coffee now."

"Get used to it, Trey. Her mother was like that too." The Chief smiled at a private memory.

Trey drank his coffee and left the older man to his thoughts. Sooner than he believed possible Red returned, not only washed, but also in a change of clothes. She made Trey feel grubby. Kissing her dad on the cheek she took her coffee and sat at the table.

"Let's get to work." Red looked all business; their connection last night might have been a dream.

Following her lead Trey swiveled to face the table.

"I gather you have been checking out my conclusions."

"I had some time on my hands." The Chief smiled. "But yes, I have been checking your conclusions. It does seem the evidence in some of the cases, if not actually tainted, is too convenient. There are a couple in which the investigation began by some piece of evidence falling in our lap. The first such case is after the eleventh elimination of an offender. Looks like some bright person put together what we were doing and figured out how to manipulate the process. It doesn't necessarily mean they know the Underground is responsible for the executions."

"I think the manner in which the evidence is manipulated suggests they know to push the setup any further will mean we won't proceed." The structure of the information felt rickety in Trey's mind. He was still missing important pieces. "Looking at cases where there was no agreement on the verdict will probably turn up early attempts. I'm wondering if Councilor Molloy was a test case to see if we would tackle someone of that political stature, as well as removing him as a roadblock to rapid change."

"Our problem is there is no indication in the media or on the net that Molloy is dead. In fact there was a story last night about him insulting the Japanese delegation by missing a personal appearance and showing up by vid link." The Chief played with his empty coffee cup.

"Vid links can be faked." Trey rubbed at his forehead trying to drag something more out of the information. "I'd be on the watch for a few more stories about Councilor Molloy in the news before he fades into the background again. It's unclear whether the people controlling the Molloy sim are the same people who are trying to manipulate the Underground. The fact the Molloy we killed was artificial makes it even murkier. Someone may have been sending the Councilor a message. In that case, he would still be alive. No need to threaten a dead man."

"So what do we do?" Red asked.

"We wait and see what happens next," Trey said. "Then we try to think of a counter move; perhaps we send our evidence in to a trusted source and see what happens."

"Put a watch on the house if there isn't already. See who shows up to investigate, if anyone does,"

Red said. "Maybe give them some 'evidence' of our own."

"I think we also need to rethink our plan of attack." The Chief pushed the cup away. "If our execution of criminals against children is open to manipulation we are putting our lives in the hands of an unknown. Security will have a fit. We must prepare for the worst and assume there is a leak from our side.

"The first part of our message may have gotten through. There's been a terrific amount of activity around crimes against children coming out of Elder Justice. It seems a Methuselah named Roberta has made it a personal vendetta.

"I will run all this past the Underground Council, and we will see what strategy they generate. I'll get the word out to stop the executions by the other groups. You go back to your team and work on training. You need to be ready for anything. Put the team on alert."

Red jumped to her feet and snapped a salute.

"Yes, Chief." She spoiled it by hugging him and kissing him on the cheek. Trey just nodded. Red led him back out through the secret passage.

When they were a safe distance from the conference room, he asked her. "Why use the secret passage? They must know we were there."

"Of course they know. But this is more fun." She snuggled up to him and delivered a long kiss. "Don't you think?"

He returned her kiss with interest. After a while Red sighed.

"I think we should get back to work." She led

him back to the nondescript door, and after checking the hallway on a computer screen, let them out.

They walked back to the briefing room, occasionally brushing against each other, but trying not to hold hands out where they could be seen by the others. When they arrived at the briefing room they found Annie and Bert with a huge stack of files in front of them. Annie looked up, smirked at them and then went back to work.

With a hand squeeze, Trey left Red's side and went to work with them. They were sorting through, not just the cases in which they had rendered a judgment, but through every case they had examined since they started the Crimes against Children teams. Trey scanned them quickly and found there wasn't much new to learn about the manipulation of the Underground, but he was sickened at the variety of ways children were abused and sold.

Dan and Jimmy wandered in and took their seats. Jimmy glared at Trey as if Trey had done him personal injury. Great, it begins already. Trey deliberately took a seat down the table from Red. When she looked puzzled he nodded at Jimmy. He could see it sink into her being. Their team was beginning to break apart.

"I looked in on Lizzy." Dan said. "She is recovering well, and should be up and around within the week. It will take a little longer before she is ready for any action with the team."

"Did you check on her too?" Jimmy asked Red,

"Or were you busy?"

"She was briefing me on the situation," the Chief said rolling into the room. "As a result of Trey's findings and some anomalies from the last mission the Council is suspending the Crimes against Children effort. Until we come up with an alternative strategy, I would like you to brainstorm about how we carry our work to the next level.

"In the meantime we are going to do some restructuring of the teams. Trey, you will head up a research and information division. Annie and Bert are cleared to help you find whatever information you need, short of knowledge of other Undergrounds. They will also put you in contact with our intelligence people.

"Red and Dan, you will look at tactics with input from other team leaders. I want to have several different ways we can look at every possible situation. You know the kind of thing I want.

"Jimmy, join the group going through our physical security. I want doors intruders will find very hard to crack yet not slow our own people significantly. Red and Trey, you'll report directly to me. I'll be your liaison with the Council."

Trey watched the reactions of his one-time teammates. Jimmy alternated between black looks at Trey and self-satisfied smugness. It wasn't a pretty combination. Annie and Bert looked relieved, Dan thoughtful. Red looked rebellious. Trey hoped she wasn't going to argue. He caught her eye and gave her a slight nod. She tilted her head at him and shrugged. She left with Dan and the Chief to look up the other team leaders. Trey and his fellow researchers put their heads together to talk about what information he needed next. He felt Jimmy hovering at his back.

"Not quite what you expected, smart boy." Trey refused to look, but his stomach sank to a familiar place. "I guess you were hoping to get assigned together and get all lovey-dovey. Too bad she's going to be too busy to even look at you."

"Don't you have work to do?" Bert's voice was curt. Jimmy huffed and slammed out of the room.

"Poor boy. It must be terrible to be so consumed with possessiveness." Annie sighed and then straightened. "Well, he will have to find his own road." She looked sharply at Trey. "The Chief is smart putting you on different teams, but Jimmy is right. You won't be seeing much of her until she gets a handle on the tactical situation."

"Red is her own person," Trey said. "She will set her own priorities. I would like to be part of them, but that's her choice. I'm thinking I will have a few questions about the computer setup."

Bert slapped his shoulder, and they began to work.

The work was hard and all consuming. Trey found excuses to look up Red and get her help with the computers and outside searches, but he found her withdrawn. He tried to coax a smile from her and once tried to steal a kiss. She just shook her head. The hardest thing Trey had ever done was to go back to treating her as just his team leader. In the meantime he pulled together more information about the

Underground and its influence on the outside society. The more he learned the more concerned he became.

A few days after the teams were rearranged Trey met Lizzy in a deserted hallway.

"Hi, Lizzy. It's good to see you up and about." Trey wasn't expecting to be pushed up against the wall and have one of her razor sharp knives at his throat.

"You were kissing Red," she rasped. "Now Red is sad."

"I kissed Red, when she wanted me to. Now she doesn't want to be kissed. I'm sad too."

"You want to kiss her?"

"Yes, Lizzy, I want to kiss her, but I have to wait for her to want it too. I think she's sad because she thinks it's getting in the way of being a leader."

"If you hurt her, I will kill you."

"If I hurt Red, I will give you the knife myself."

Lizzy thought for a moment and took the knife away.

"I'll be watching you."

"Look after Red, Lizzy. She needs you."

Trey watched Lizzy walk away as if they had just been discussing the weather outside. Whatever had been done to her, it had destroyed her ability to understand emotions, even her own. She was probably more dangerous now than she had ever been. Yet Trey could understand her a little. She was even more an outsider than he was. Cursed to live forever in a child's body with memories no one should have to own.

"Live forever!" Trey slapped his head. "How stupid could I be?" He headed toward his office at a run.

He typed in search parameters. Life extension, artificial bodies, immortality. Most of what came up was rumor and nonsense but he persisted. Every time he hit a roadblock he wished he had Red and her hacking skills, but then he would find another way to the information. By the end of the day he still had only guesswork, but he persisted. There was an answer in there somewhere.

"I am not sure we can avoid open conflict," he reported to the Chief a week later. "The path we're on is leading us both further away from the geritocracy ruling outside, and setting us up as a competing ideal for society. The elders can't rule and allow us to challenge the very basis for their rule. Right now we serve two functions for them.

"First, we are a safety valve. The discontented join us and think they are striking a blow against the oppressive regime. In reality most of the members of the Underground are living very similar lives to what they would outside. Most of our people are on contracts, just as the rest of the outsiders. Because we tell them they are gathering information for us doesn't change the reality they are strengthening the present economy by their efforts.

"Second, all the really dangerous people are gathered in one place. By allowing the Underground to continue, all the people with the energy and the will to cause trouble for the government are centralized. I'm wondering if the attempt to subtly influence the Underground to further polarize the issues is not a precursor to some move the Elders' Council, or someone on it, thinks will cause general unrest. Someone is trying to set us up to take the fall for further oppression of the young." He opened his mouth to mention his research into immortality then closed it. He didn't have enough yet. "To get any further, I will need someone with Red's skills on the computer."

Trey waited carefully. The long silence that followed wasn't a good omen.

"I told you Red is her own woman." The Chief shook his head. "I don't want to get involved again. I broke up the teams partly to give you young people a chance without getting into trouble for being in the same chain of command. Some of the Council members are sticklers for protocol. It seems to have backfired on you, and I am sorry."

"She blames our relationship for breaking up the team. So she is retreating into her duty, and trying to avoid repeating her mistake." Trey shrugged. "It doesn't change the fact I need her skills to do my work. I will send Annie to be the liaison between Intelligence and Tactics. She knows what I need, and she won't be such a distraction."

"Did anyone ever tell you, you are too smart for your own good?"

"Several times, sir, several times." Trey got up and left to find Annie to brief her.

"Good luck, son," the Chief said as Trey closed the door.

Busted

Jimmy sat at his computer console and sulked. He couldn't understand how Red would choose that helpless brainiac over him. The wuss wouldn't last twenty minutes outside. Jimmy kicked the desk. *It wasn't fair.* He was the one who kept going back to the street and taking all the real risks. All Trey did was sit and think.

Jimmy had spent the last few days with the security team retooling all the locks to the doors outside. They were all controlled by a central system isolated from the rest of the network. Even if someone did hack into the Underground's system, they wouldn't have access to the doors. Jimmy suggested they take the idea a step further and put other selected doors under the computer control, ones which could be used to direct or control traffic to certain parts of the underground. He put regulators on some of the doors in the training area. The brain was going to get a shock the next time the team trained.

Only they wouldn't be training anymore. The

Chief had broken up the team. It was all Trey's fault. All Jimmy wanted was for Red to look at him the way she looked at Trey. He wanted the feel of her hand in his. That wasn't too much to ask was it? He wiped his eyes and looked at the monitor. There he was just wandering around without caring he had destroyed Jimmy's world. If Trey hadn't come along, Red would have fallen for Jimmy. He just knew it.

Jimmy watched Trey walking in an area with the new door protocols. His computer was hooked into the separate control network for the new security systems. It was only temporary while Jimmy checked out the status of the changes. Maybe he should do some testing. He pulled a schematic up on another screen and locked a few doors. Trey tried one door then another. Jimmy laughed at the expression on Trey's face. He used the system to push Trey toward one particular door. This was one even the security team didn't know about. It was Jimmy's personal exit. By now Trey was frantically trying every door and running back and forth like a scared rabbit. Jimmy laughed so hard his stomach hurt.

Trey found Jimmy's special door, and went through it. Jimmy couldn't see him once he left the Underground, but he could imagine the panic on Trey's face. He wasn't so smart now. There was an entrance not too far from the tunnel Trey was in. If he was half as smart as he thought he was, Trey would be able to find his way back inside in a few minutes. Jimmy switched the camera to the entrance and watched. He wanted to see the bastard's face when he came crawling back. Jimmy was so intent on the monitor he didn't see the message scrolling across the bottom of the screen.

Updated security protocols in place; new passes are necessary to unlock any Underground access point from the outside. Security personnel at exits points are to double check all passes to make sure they are current.

Jimmy watched for an hour, then two. He went from feeling smug to uncertain to panic. If they caught him playing with security protocols he would be in deep trouble. Even so, Jimmy considered going to his section chief to tell him Trey had got locked out. But then he would have to explain about his door, and he knew where that would go. Instead Jimmy went through the log and carefully erased all trace of his activity. Then he cut the computer he was using from the security net.

"Sorry," Jimmy said, "You're on your own now." He wasn't sure, but he might even *feel* sorry. Jimmy shrugged and left the room. There were things he could be doing.

***

After talking to Annie, Trey went looking for Red. Even if she wouldn't talk to him, he wanted to look at her. Then he changed his mind and went down to the training section. He would just go for a run and work himself to exhaustion. Trey ran along the hallways until he was thirsty. There was a room up ahead with a sink in it. He could get a drink there. The door was locked. He jogged on to another room, but that room was locked too. Trey decided he'd had enough running and turned to go back, but the fire doors, which were never closed, were not only closed, but locked.

He worked his way around another way to get out of the training area, but when the second and third sets of fire doors also wouldn't budge he began to panic. He tried door after door until finally one opened. It slammed shut behind him before he fully realized he was out in the unsecured tunnels. Trey tried the door he had just gone through, but it was locked tight. He stopped to think for a moment while he caught his breath. He went through the pattern of what just happened and an answer floated up. Jimmy worked with the security detail; he was probably playing with Trey, trying to make him panic. It had almost worked.

Trey knew where he was in reference to the Underground. The closest door wasn't far. He walked to it. Like the fire doors it refused to open. His pass still sat in his pants pocket. He didn't feel like waiting for someone to notice him standing outside the door, not to mention he risked being seen on the outside security net if the cameras weren't being redirected.

The closest door with security staff he could talk to was at a mall service corridor. He was taking a risk going topside without anything disguising his appearance, but it should be a quick walk; late enough not many people would be outside, early enough he didn't think he'd have trouble with curfew. Better than going around to the main doors and begging to be let in. Trey set off at a jog toward where he expected an exit would be. When he got back in, he'd memorize these tunnels as he had the

Underground.

Before long he felt a breath of fresh air, and decided to follow it. Once he was up top he'd be only a few minutes from getting back inside. Trey found the exit – a ladder up to an overflow. The bars had rusted away and he could easily slip through.

The cold air made Trey turn his collar up as he walked. He needed to find a cross street to tell him the fastest way to the access at the mall. He came to a corner and didn't pay much attention when he rounded it. The growl chilled him worse than the wind. A dogbot stood just a short distance away from him, its eyes glowing red. Trey stood still and waited for it to wander away. Instead it moved forward and backed him up against the wall. He heard a siren approaching rapidly in the distance. Trey spent the time fixing his story in his mind before the police arrived. Good thing he'd been wearing the shoes without the lock-picks under the sole. The pass looked like a library card, and it no longer worked anyway.

Trey set his face in as sullen an expression as he could manage as the local police pulled up. He didn't need to fake the shivering, and he had carefully scrubbed his face with his hands to make himself grimier. It all depended on whether they were looking for a desperate rebel or just picking up a wandering youth who had broken curfew.

The police didn't give him any clues. They silently and efficiently searched him, put cuffs on him, and transported him to the local station.

At the station, Trey got his first clue this wasn't a random arrest. As they processed his fingerprints and

DNA he could see the reflection of a red warning flag on the computer screen in the Sergeant's glasses.

The police still did their work in silence, except for their orders to him, but he could sense they were waiting for him to try something. The little he had learned from Dan wasn't going to help him escape a room full of cops eager to subdue him. He was careful to do exactly what he was told.

They left him in a cold bare cell in the basement. There was no one else down there. Trey sat on the bed and considered his options. He knew far too much about the Underground to allow anyone to interrogate him. He had no illusions about his ability to fight the drugs and psychological techniques they would use. Unfortunately the police had efficiently stripped him of anything he could use to kill himself. The worst part was Red would think he had just deserted them for no reason.

Tears threatened at the back of his eyes and he fought them by going into his analytic mode. What would the Underground do? They'd have to abandon the facility. Trey would single-handedly bring down the Underground.

He was wondering if he could break his neck by running into the wall when there was a commotion at the other end of the corridor. The gate to the holding block was thrown open and someone was ushered into the cellblock. The muted voices of the police held both fear and reverence. Trey recognized the man from the file on him in the Chief's office, but even without that he would have remembered those cold eyes.

Methuselah Grant walked up to Trey's cell and stood in front of it leaning on a cane. He didn't say anything but the local cops scurried to unlock the door and bring a chair for the old man. He looked around and nodded. The locals disappeared in seconds, leaving Trey alone with the man who had destroyed his family.

"So, where has your father been hiding you, boy?" The question was so far from what Trey expected he could only stare at the old man. "Don't play stupid with me, boy. I have seen your test scores. Now where has your father been hiding you?" He jabbed Trey with the cane. "I don't have all day." Trey was used to his thoughts moving at blazing speed, but the distance between reality and his assumptions made his thoughts crawl as if he waded through molasses.

"I haven't seen my Dad since you took me away," Trey finally stammered.

"Nonsense, you are far too important to be allowed to just wander around." The old man sounded as if Trey was deliberately making his life hard. "How did he contact you at the Reserve? Who did he have helping him?" With each question the Methuselah jabbed Trey a little harder.

"I ran away from the Reserve. My father had nothing to do with it, unless you count bringing me into the world in the first place."

"Exactly. What are your father's plans for you?" The next jab of the cane was accompanied by a jolt of electricity. Trey shouted and pulled back. "It can get a lot worse, boy."

"I don't know what my father wants from me. He never told me. He never talked to me since you dragged me away from his side. I always thought I was his organ bank."

"I had wondered about that at first, but now I don't know. It doesn't seem subtle enough for Mulholland. He had something more in mind." He poked Trey again, sending another jolt through his body. "You are going to tell me everything you know. Beginning with what your father told you."

"My father didn't tell me anything. He took me to the zoo; we walked in the park. I was a KID you stupid old coot." It wasn't a jolt this time, it was a full blown blast of power shooting up and down all Trey's nerves and leaving him twitching uncontrollably on the floor.

"You probably won't die, but I can make you wish you had."

"I don't have the answers you want. It doesn't matter how many times you zap me, I still won't know."

"Then it will be a long night for both of us." The Methuselah stopped asking questions and just prodded at Trey. Sometimes he would apply the shock, sometimes not. He finally left Trey lying soaking wet on the cement.

"I do believe I will leave you here for a time. There is too much...paperwork involved with bringing you to Justice."

"What...would...you...know...about...justice... old...fart."

The old man looked at Trey for a long time, then shook his head and walked away.

The locals came and complained about the mess, but Trey couldn't make his voice work well enough to respond. They moved him to the next cell and left him on the naked mattress. One of them ran a quick mop through the mess he'd made, then tossed a set of bright orange coveralls at him.

"Damned if I'm going to change you, kid." He followed the others out and Trey was once again alone with his thoughts.

THE RESCUE

Red didn't know what to do with herself. She desperately wanted to spend time with Trey. Banter with Trey had become how she de-stressed when the world became too real. She reviewed how he had been careful to ask Lizzy's permission while questioning her, and he did it without knowing anything about Lizzy. He was sensitive and caring, so much more than just a brain. Life after the revolution felt possible because of him.

Her body wanted to lose itself in his arms. But she couldn't. She had responsibilities. People depended on her. A few minutes of carelessness had caused her father to break up her team. Since he'd seen her and Trey together, Jimmy had turned into a different person - one minute being the young scamp she had rescued, the next minute giving her the creeps.

She threw herself into the work of developing an alternative tactic to eliminating those who viewed children as property. She talked scenarios over with Dan and the leaders of the other teams. They were all older than her, but listened carefully. It was heady stuff.

The newscast still mentioned Councilor Molloy almost every day in reference to one thing or another.

She'd sent a squad out to watch the house. There had been no new activity other than truly desperate people searching for anything to loot. The Underground's agent had managed to plant some evidence with the Methuselah who had roared in to push everyone around. He'd taken the bait and refused the hook. There wasn't the slightest rumor of an investigation against Councilor Molloy. She brought the agent inside to keep her safe in case Justice decided to ask her more questions. The girl did say the Methuselah wasn't the normal 'hate all young people' type.

The janitor had turned up dead the day after the fiasco of Molloy's execution. That fit with Trey's theory they were being used. The theory infuriated her. Not Trey's fault, but every time she thought about Trey, she remembered someone had been using the Underground as their own personal hit squad and kicked herself for not seeing it. If she hadn't let herself be distracted then she might have. Then she started missing him all over again. Maybe her father was right; she didn't have the focus to be a good team leader.

She sat with four other team leaders studying plans she had of the Elder Justice building. The plans were old and outdated but they were the best they had. There were large blank sections in the plans as well. Red and the others were trying to figure out what was in the gaps. They hadn't got much past agreeing the holding cells were probably in the basement. There was a lot of plumbing for an office building. Red suspected the security was beyond anything she could imagine.

The Chief rolled up the plans and pushed them to one side.

"Enough of that," he said. "We are likely never making a frontal assault on the Elder Justice building. We do need to put some plans in place for different tactical situations here. The advantage is we have detailed plans for our own turf."

Red unrolled a series of plans covering the entire table. The man who'd built the place ages ago must have been a riot to work with. Everything was mapped in detail. The first trick to using the maps was learning to ignore the excess information. She tapped on the plans.

"You will have to imagine they are stacked up in three dimensions. What we need to do is have escape routes and attack vectors, and ways to keep them separate."

"We could use doors to move the attackers in the direction we want them." One of the security leads said. "We're already working on it. The escape routes are going to be harder. Anyone with minimal competence will have the place surrounded. Even if we can avoid the attackers, the escapees will run into the perimeter." He pointed to the exits marked on the plans. "If we have a leak, we can't guarantee any safe routes. We might want to start evacuating now, but it would tip our hand to whoever's out there.

"We could use a distraction. Have something set up, and trigger it in case of attack." Another team leader, who worked mostly with the Middlers peered at the plans. "Given enough confusion we could slip people past the attackers, especially if we're herding them about."

They batted the pros and cons of the ideas back and forth, fingers drawing lines on the plans, but didn't arrive at any firm conclusions.

"Those are all good ideas. I would like you to develop them further. We meet here same time tomorrow." The Chief waved them out.

Red nodded to the others, and left. She had been delighted to discover the older team leaders took her completely in stride. They didn't cut her any slack, but they treated each member of the group the same way. It was almost a relief to not be the one in charge.

Time to find Trey. She'd been blaming him for her own mistakes. Red thought dreamily about what would happen after she apologized. He wasn't in the old briefing room that he used with Annie and Bert. He wasn't in his quarters either. Her Dad said Trey had left him a couple of hours before. She'd look up Lizzy and let Trey stew for a while. Lizzy was back at her post at the front door to the Council offices. She gave Red an odd look, but didn't say anything.

They talked until Red found herself yawning. She wandered back to her room, checking on Trey's room one more time. He was still not there, not at the briefing room either, but Annie was.

"Hey, Red, could you run a quick search? Trey wanted to know how many dogbots were in the area, and how effective they might be in assisting an attack. He also wanted to know how many people had access to living quarters outside of the Underground. Last thing he wanted was the retirement rates for the local police forces. I know it's one ugly group of searches, but that's Trey for you."

Red nodded and sat down at the computer. She signed on with a back door, which had been leaked to the Underground, and started looking at dogbot activity. What she found froze her with fingers over the keyboard.

"Trey got outside somehow. He's been arrested. They took him to the local police holding cells and he still seems to be there. I don't think he'll be there long. With the people who are looking for him, he will be moved to Elder Justice soon." Red found she was trembling. She wanted to break something. No, *someone.*

"He wouldn't have gone outside deliberately," Annie said.

"Jimmy," Red said, "the jealous little punk, this is just the thing he would pull."

"Not Lizzy?"

"If Lizzy was mad at him, he would be dead, not busted." She bashed the keyboard. "Find Jimmy and confine him to quarters. I don't think he's going to betray the Underground. He probably just thought he was playing a joke on Trey. I want his team checked with a microscope. Anyone you don't trust, lock them up. Send Bert for Dan, and I'll want Lizzy too."

"Aren't you overreacting a bit? We've had people arrested before."

"Not like Trey. He knows enough to blow the whole underground. Let's just hope he can hold out until we get there. Go, quickly."

Annie left at a run. Red was already pulling up screens and looking at plans for the local cells. Her father came in.

"Are you sure about this?"

"We can't leave him there. He knows too much." Red looked at her father. He just looked back at her. "I can't do it, Dad, I love him. I can't just walk away."

"Do what you need to do, Red." He kissed her on the forehead. "Whatever you need, just ask." He turned as he reached the door. "You'll want to take him to a safe house. Bring Lizzy with you."

After he left Red went back to the plans. They were in luck and a major storm drain ran beside the cells. Red pulled up the weather. There was a chance of heavy rains. She thought that might be to their advantage. People started arriving in the briefing room. Jimmy came in too. Red had to restrain herself. She wanted to tear his eyes out.

"Red...I'm sorry." Jimmy looked terrified almost on the point of tears. "I was just going to play with him. I didn't think he would go topside."

"When did you ever think this was a game?" Red leaned over him.

"But..."

"No buts. You may have doomed us with your petty game. You can apologize after we have Trey back. So stay quiet unless you have something to contribute or you go back to quarters with a guard on your door."

"I'll do anything..." Jimmy stammered to halt. Every pair of eyes in the room looked at him with the same expression.

The last people arrived and she put the little punk out of her mind.

"Here is the plan..."

They split up to pick up the gear they needed while Red laid down a map through the maze of tunnels to the spot they were going to attack.

"I've been in those cells," Jimmy spoke hardly above a whisper. "They like to put prisoners in the far end to keep the noise and smell down. You'll want to blow the wall as far from the cells as we can manage."

Red nodded curtly and looked at Dan who managed the explosives.

She picked up her tablet and linked into the tunnel network. A few taps set the cameras and sensors to reporting the activity from a few hours ago, mostly rats scurrying in the dark.

Dan led them into the tunnels. Red carried her tablet, and her fingers twitched to break into the cells' camera network, but it would be too risky. Justice would have Trey watched real-time. Someone would spot her.

They stopped by a blank section of wall. She double-checked their position relative to the cells. She tapped on a spot and Dan started placing explosives.

"It's going to be messy in there," Red ground the words out past the fear gnawing at her throat. "We get in, grab Trey and get out. Dan will leave a unexploded device on the wall to make them think we've booby trapped the tunnels. Remember, I'm redirecting as much rainwater as I can into the tunnels, so you'll want to hit the surface as quick as you can after we're done. Stay calm and don't raise any flags. Annie, Bert, you keep eyes on Jimmy."

Dan gave her a thumbs up and stepped away from the wall.

"Let's go," she said. They pulled masks over their faces and prepared for the blast.

***

Trey was trying to sleep through the twitches remaining from the Methuselah's visit when the wall at the end of the cells blew in and dust and smoke filled the place. He pulled the coveralls to his face and tried to breathe through the fabric.

Black masked people poured into the corridor at one end while local police poured in through the other. Canisters rolled down the hall spewing even more smoke and gas. He heard a shot before coughing and gasping enveloped the police end of the cells.

One of the masked figures knelt at the door to Trey's cell and fumbled with the lock. Trey staggered to his feet and headed toward the door. A police officer grabbed the person trying to pick the lock. Trey reached through the bars to grab at the cop, but fell against them instead. Another tiny figure stormed out of the smoke and leveled the cop. He'd seen her in action enough to know exactly who it was.

When he tried to say something the gas choked his throat closed until he could barely grunt. Jimmy finished with the lock and Lizzy sent him back into the smoke with a none-too-gentle smack. She pulled the door open and strong arms guided him back toward the gaping hole in the wall.

Police in gas masks rushed them. One of his rescuers stood in their way. Trey knew her stance too.

"Go. I've got this." Dan stepped past them and sank into the 'ready' position. Dan's hands and feet blurred as he sent the closest cops reeling back with gas masks torn off or askew. He dropped another canister as Trey was pushed through the hole.

Past the hole in the wall people ran off in all directions. Red and Lizzy wrapped his arms around them and half walked, half dragged him to one of the wheeled platforms he had seen the first day he met Red. He was dropped on the platform and squeezed in between the two. Between the smoke and the exhaustion from the jolts he'd taken he closed his eyes and once again, remembered nothing of the ride.

***

He woke up in a strange bed with a warm body beside him. For something so completely new, it felt absolutely right. He rolled over to find Red looking at him. Something in her gaze froze him in place. After a long moment she grinned and kissed him on the nose.

"Uhh..."

"Is that all you have to say?" Red kissed him

181

again.

"You always manage to take my breath away."

"You certainly know how to make a girl feel good."

Trey turned red, then noticed he was still dressed in the orange coveralls.

"How?"

"Well, I wasn't going to let you sleep in your other clothes. We gave you a shower and put you back in those hideous things."

"Shower? We?" Trey felt his face get even hotter.

Lizzy waved at him from the chair where she was curled up like a cat.

"Why do I sleep through all the best parts?" he moaned.

"What?" Red squealed. She elbowed him and he fell to the floor. "Do you know how hard it is to wash someone who is sleeping on their feet? And then poor Lizzy stayed up all night to protect my virtue, and you didn't even try to cuddle, you just snored away." She made snores sounding more like a pig than any human noise. Trey caught her foot as it poked his ribs, and pulled her on top of him.

"Having a shower with you is something I want to remember," he said into her eyes. "Just like waking up beside you is a memory I will cherish forever. I love you, even though I am not quite sure what it means, and I am prepared to spend the rest of my life with you figuring it out." Red didn't reply, just kissed him until he thought he would burst. Then she hugged him and cried into his shoulder.

"I think that's the nicest thing anyone has ever said to me," she said. "But I don't know what Lizzy will make of all this."

Lizzy just shrugged. Trey sat against the wall and pulled Red so she was leaning against him. Tilting her head back she kissed him again. Lizzy rolled her eyes, but smiled at the two of them.

"A Methuselah came to see me in the cells." Trey said after he'd absorbed enough of Red's warmth to set his mind going.

"Which one?"

"The one with the dead eyes. He took me away from my father. He asked all the wrong questions."

"What do you mean wrong questions?" Red tried to peer at him from where she leaned in his arms, but gave up and twisted around.

"I was all ready to lie to him about the Underground, but it was like he didn't care we existed. Everything was about my father. How did he contact me? Where did he hide me? What was I supposed to be? I didn't know, so he kept shocking me with his cane."

"His cane?"

"Yeah, he would jab me with his cane and hit a button and 'pow!' I would be twitching all over. Even after he knew I was clueless he kept zapping me. For fun I guess."

"No," Lizzy said, "to make you afraid, and to plant a locator."

"Not too deep fortunately, we got it out and a crew of street kids is meandering through the city trading it off."

"We may want it back at some point," Trey said. "It could be useful to draw them to a place of our choice. Back to the questions, if he didn't ask about the Underground, it may mean he already thinks he knows enough."

"I'll message the Chief." Lizzy handed Red her tablet. When she put it down again, Trey sighed and slumped more against the wall.

"Red, I need to talk to my father. If that Methuselah is so interested in me and my father, then I can't ignore it."

Red sighed. "Right now?"

"Soon," Trey said. "If he was willing to torture me for answers, then we need those answers to stop him."

"OK," said Red. "Let's find your dad."

Watch and Learn

Joe walked into his office that morning to find Devon waiting for him.

"There were some very interesting things going on last night."

Joe raised his eyebrow.

"Trey was apprehended by the local police yesterday while out wandering down by the river. They brought him to a local station and processed him. Methuselah Grant showed up and questioned him rather severely since it appears they had to change cells to clean up. Their records clerk is very particular. Shortly after they had moved the young man, a gang of thugs broke in through the wall with explosives and carried him away. One shot was fired, by the police, but no one appears to have been hit. A great deal of various smoke and gas bombs was used. By the time the air cleared the gang had vanished into the tunnels. The heavy rains flooded the tunnels and made a search impossible. The locals are searching now with dogbots and scanners, but have turned up nothing."

"I would love to know what he thought he would learn from Trey." Joe absently went through the process of making coffee.

"A number of complaints a year or so back about the local police treatment of prisoners resulted in the installation of surveillance cameras in the cell blocks. I don't know if they are effective in preventing police brutality, but a tape showed up as evidence in a recent trial. The defendant had been held in the same cells as Trey."

"See what you can find." Joe went into his office and sat down to think. Things were heating up. Trey must be very important to the resistance if they were showing their hand by breaking into a police station. They were obviously using the tunnels for their operations. He pulled up a map of service tunnels and drains on his computer. They ran through the whole city. He had always taken the city services for granted without thinking too much about how people worked on them. If the resistance followers were living in the tunnels they had access to the entire city. It also made them vulnerable to gas attacks.

Devon brought in the morning coffee. They drank it in silence, but Joe set his aside after a few minutes. He could see fire in his assistant's eyes. It was reminiscent of the look on Maggie's face just before she quit.

"OK, Devon. What's on your mind?"

"Let me show you the video I downloaded." He tapped a few keys and Joe was watching Trey sitting in his cell staring at the wall. The camera was mounted so one camera could cover as many cells as possible, but Joe could clearly see the young man staring at the wall. Some noise came from off screen and Trey turned his head. The locals escorted a Methuselah in, brought a chair, then left. Joe immediately recognized Grant. Even if he couldn't see the face he would recognize the arrogant stance.

Joe watched the opening exchange of questions and saw the bewildered look on Trey's face. He saw and listened to the whole sequence, ending with Trey twitching on the bed. The locals returned and moved him to a different cell, then sluiced down the old one. Within minutes of them leaving, there was a bang and the corridor was filled with dust and smoke. He listened to the confusion. Two masked figures helped Trey out of his cell and Joe froze the frame.

"What color hair is on the left hand person?"

"It looks blue. A lot of young people dye their hair."

"Print the frame and send it to the lab. They have a couple of hair samples I would like them to compare the color as best they can." Devon nodded, but didn't immediately leave the office. "You might want to make a copy of the tape and have it ready. I don't want to muddy the waters just yet, but as far as a Methuselah's powers go, I don't believe they extend to the torture of children. We will want to be sure someone can follow up on that tape." Devon looked defiant for a moment then nodded.

"I will archive it so no one but I can find it."

"If the rebels are using the tunnels, why has no one found them yet?"

"There are a lot of tunnels, the cameras and other sensors would report to a computer, not a person. It wouldn't be difficult to break into the network and redirect security feeds to where ever they wanted. I could do it if I needed to, and I'm not the best hacker around."

"So the police would think the tunnels clear and not bother with physical patrols."

"Very likely. Easier to act on what you think you know than ask too many questions."

"Very good," Joe tapped on his desk. "Do an analysis to determine whether Councilor Molloy's position on any issues has shifted in the last week or so. If someone is running Molloy's ghost, I would like to know what they are up to."

Devon nodded again, and this time he left.

Joe was still deep in thought when the lab buzzed to say the blue hair from the trunk of the car at the fire scene could not be matched exactly to the frame in the video, but they were not entirely different colors. They also said there were several odd markers on the DNA on the hair. They estimated the owner of the hair to be in the fifty to eighty year old range.

Joe thanked them and went back to thinking. Assume Molloy was attracted to children for whatever twisted reason. The old woman at the house had said they carried out a *child* covered in blood. Either the hairs were from a different person than had been carried out of the house, or there was someone who looked like a child who was over fifty years old.

He pulled up his computer and ran a search. Sure enough about fifty-five years ago a lab was closed down for doing illegal gene experimentation on children. According to the case notes they had been trying to freeze aging at some 'optimum' age. Several test subjects had been taken into custody, but not one was still living. There was always the possibility of a backdoor deal to increase funding. These labs and their desperate experiments to stop aging were almost as pervasive as the people who used children for their own pleasure. Joe didn't think either was an indication of a healthy society.

He had started this case with his normal hard-nosed attitude that all people were deserving of fair treatment. Anyone who took liberties with the life of another person could expect Joe to show up asking questions and dealing out his own form of justice. He had thought, because the people around him were of a like mind, most of society must be as well. Maggie, and now Devon challenged him because he wasn't doing enough! And they were right. There was something basically wrong with the society he took for granted. Trey called it a geritocracy – rule by the old. Being old didn't automatically grant extra wisdom. The people running the country were using their position to try to stave off death. No wonder Grant assumed Mulholland had some nefarious purpose in having Trey, because that's what the Methuselah would do.

It wasn't quite a crime to be young, but the young were disadvantaged in every way conceivable. They were locked into long contracts - the next best thing to indentured servitude. If they were fortunate enough to live to eighty they would discover retirement was a dream only for the rich, for the rest it was the Homes. As hard as some folks tried, the Homes were more nightmare than dream.

As Grant was fond of saying, life wasn't fair. The problem was Grant had stopped trying to make it fair. Joe feared he was heading down the same path. If he really was going to make a difference he would need to go after the powerful who were abusing their power to subjugate the poor.

Devon came back into the room.

"I finished the analysis you asked for. The only thing Molloy has made the slightest shift on is identity rights. He has always been one for 'You get one body, and you had better take care of it because it is the only one you are going to get.' Now he has moved to support mandatory donation for criminals, and even the possibility identity doesn't rest with the body."

"Interesting, the forensics people found evidence of an anomaly, suggesting a construct. It would also explain why he still looked like his old self. He didn't want to appear to be in contradiction of his position. So who does this shift help?"

"It helps Molloy, if he made a copy of himself. It's theoretically possible, but the computing power need is enormous. He might leave out things he thought unnecessary, though what it would do to your mental health is beyond me. We are as much emotions and hormones as we are thought."

"So you are suggesting we should look for increasing shifts in policy and perhaps an over-rational approach..."

"Possibly, or we could be grasping at straws. Someone else could be running Molloy's sim to their own advantage."

"How long could they stay accurate to people who actually know him? The two cent council is an absolutely exclusive group. They would be hard to fool for long."

"Not if the person had access to files Molloy created in hopes of creating a backup. They would have all the information, if not necessarily the personality."

"So we watch for personality shifts as well?" Joe got up to pace. He tried to imagine being in a different body, but failed. Creaky as it might be, this body was him as much as his mind.

"They might show up quicker than policy shifts, but either scenario could produce personality changes by running a robot sim. They'd need him to change to make sense of policy shifts. Whether the change is someone changing programing or that living in an artificial body is driving him insane."

"Have we really come to this? Measuring a man's words to decide if he is still himself or insane or someone else? Now we are morally bankrupt looking for the final excuse to steal the life of the young to keep the old alive."

"I wonder if that's what Grant thinks Mulholland

has in mind. A clone would be a perfect candidate for a full body transplant. The only thing holding them back is the rejection issue. If Trey were a clone of Mulholland he could receive the brain and brain stem without any drugs." Joe stopped pacing to look at Devon.

"You said Trey's DNA was slightly different."

"Perhaps to fix some genetic error Mulholland sees in himself, but not enough to prevent a transplant."

"Do you think Mulholland plans a transplant?"

"No, Mulholland doesn't strike me as someone who is looking for the key to his immortality. There *is* something important about Trey, but nothing as simple as being spare parts. Grant's problem is he can't handle subtle, or he would have noticed he was asking the wrong questions." Joe started pacing again.

"So are we asking the right questions?"

"Probably not, but we need to keep asking until we get to them."

"So here's another question. Why has the Child Crimes Killer stopped?" Devon looked at Joe and waited.

"Stopped? There is usually some time between deaths. It hasn't been long."

"There are indications the killings were the work of a group operating across the country. You've said so yourself. Some deaths occurred in different jurisdictions virtually simultaneously. They've stopped."

"All of them?" Joe leaned back to think. "If we could find out if the killers were being manipulated to some end, I'm sure they could draw the same conclusions. I would very much doubt a rebellion would appreciate being used as an assassination squad for an unknown group."

"You seem pretty sure about the rebellion." Devon was almost balanced on his toes as if the conversation led to uncomfortable ideas.

"There have always been people who didn't like the way things are. I suspect lately the dissatisfaction has become organized. The Child Crime Murders may have been a way to try to force change without resorting to open warfare." Joe dropped back into his chair.

"It doesn't bother you there is a group of people who have dedicated themselves to destroying the government?"

"If I thought that was all they were about, but the targets aren't major political figures, they're criminals." Joe leaned back and watched his secretary. Something was going on there, more than general concern for the country.

"And if the two were combined?" Now Devon paced through Joe's office.

"Councilor Molloy. Funny how many trails lead back to our Councilor. The replacements for the victims might have been chosen for the sole purpose of making life harder for the young. Adding to the dissatisfaction could incite violence. Would open rebellion help anyone?"

"If the government wanted to enforce even stricter laws, a rebellion would play right into the government's hands." Devon froze and glared at

Joe.

"But hundreds of people could die." Joe's stomach almost rebelled at the thought.

"That doesn't seem to be a concern for Molloy, or the person behind him. People die every day. What's a few more in the cause of good government?"

"You sound like you sympathize with them." Joe said.

Devon met Joe's stare for a brief moment, then sighed.

"Anyone who is poor and young might sympathize with them." He got up. "If you will excuse me, I have some work to do."

He walked out of the office leaving Joe staring at the door. Devon may or may not sympathize with the rebellion, but Joe had discovered to his horror he did. Now he had to decide what to do about it.

MEETING WITH DAD

Red and Trey untangled themselves reluctantly and joined Lizzy at a rickety kitchen table. They drank potent coffee to wake them up. But even awake, an emotional umbilical joined them. To Red's surprise their special bond didn't get in the way of their planning; instead it meant each of them needed to explain less. Lizzy just listened as she always did. She nodded a few times, and shook her head once.

Red checked in with the Chief and learned everyone had made it back safely. He'd kept the high alert since roving patrols moved through the tunnels looking for the slightest indication of use. As many people as possible were staying in alternate places up top to make the Underground a more difficult target. Security had found the mole - a computer tech whose mother had been placed in a Home. She'd been bought with the promise to move her mom to a better facility. New communication protocols had tripped her up. Now she sat in a secure room.

Trey researched his father. For the first time since

the Methuselah had dragged him screaming from his father's side, he thought about what he would ask. The problem with being a genius was you tended to assume you were right all the time. Trey didn't want his assumptions to get in the way of talking to his father about what was going on. He still felt the occasional twitch in his right hand from the cold-eyed Methuselah's questions.

Deputy Chancellor Mulholland had been promoted to D.C. shortly after Trey was removed. He served his duties in an exemplary manner, but in a government of long-lived individuals, promotion was slow. He was still Deputy Chancellor after all these years, though the area of his responsibility had grown enormously. He was now in charge of the negotiations with the contingent from Japan. They would likely still be negotiating a year from now. The very old with dreams of immortality didn't need to move quickly. Mulholland was careful, exact, and occasionally brilliant. It was generally agreed he was Chancellor in all but name. Unfortunately Chancellor O'Brien was neither in line for a promotion to the Council, nor sick enough to be expected to die soon. Mulholland would be Deputy Chancellor for the foreseeable future.

There was nothing in the research about a latecomer third son named Trey Gauche. There was no indication of Machiavellian plots around transplants or genetic experimentation. Everything Trey could uncover pointed to Mulholland being an efficient and somewhat dull civil servant. It was time to go and ask some questions, but they needed a plan to get access to him. Lowly as Deputy Chancellor might be, he still rated some pretty heavy security, not to mention the security surrounding the Japanese.

Even Red couldn't be sure of sending an email which wouldn't leave a trace to them or Mulholland. Chances were he had an assistant managing his office email, and finding his private address could set off other alarms.

So he and Red came up with a plan that was either brilliant or insane. Trey admitted it had elements of both. They worked at it until they thought they had a reasonable chance of success. The Chief made them rework it until they had built in an escape in case of failure.

It began with Red taking him to a deserted part of the city and teaching him to drive. He knew how to get a car to move from one place to another, but Red took driving to a whole new level. Like Dan's training in combat, he needed to learn a completely different set of reflexes. It took him a while to become expert enough to pass her rigorous standards. The whole exercise was so stressful they had to take a half hour break in the back of the van to cuddle and relax.

The next part was convincing Lizzy to dye her hair something other than blue. They didn't have any of her collection of wigs to hide the color. That was the one shake of the head. Lizzy's hair was blue and was going to stay blue. She did agree to cover it up with a wool cap. She and Red found some especially old and ratty clothes.

Trey learned the Japanese wanted to visit the inner city. The Council in its wisdom had decreed they would be given a modified taste of the city at its worst. The Underground had contacts in the area the contingent was visiting. That wasn't the hard part.

The hard part would be passing the Deputy Chancellor a message in front of all the security and vid cameras. It had to be a message only Mulholland would understand, but would have to be compelling enough for him to risk his career following up. The message was Trey's job; delivery was up to Red and Lizzy. After one experience with the dogbots they didn't want to chance him again. Red could read the dogbots' output, but their programming was out of reach.

The three of them piled into the van and headed toward the cordoned-off strip. Trey dropped Red and Lizzy off then parked well out of the security sweep.

***

The girls walked along the street. Red greeted everyone as if they were old friends, and she was outrageous enough to pull it off. They arrived at the corner their contacts usually staked out. Lizzy had a brief staring contest with a couple of young studs who were about to lay claim to the deserted spot. Left to themselves, it was a simple matter to arrange their gear as if they always worked on the streets. Red pulled out the cards and practiced a simple trick Jimmy had taught her. The one change in the trick was essential to Trey's message to his father.

The morning wore on and Red put away the

cards. She was confident in her ability to pull it off. She was less confident in Mulholland's ability to receive the message. Trey thought it would work and she trusted him. She spent the rest of the morning in a pleasant haze thinking about the redhead who had so precipitously entered her life. While Trey couldn't remember the platform ride or the shower, Red could. She reviewed them in a loop while Lizzy watched with a sardonic look on her face. Their stomachs were growling by the time Lizzy nudged Red to pull her out of her memories.

"Stop drooling over the boy, and get ready."

Red snorted, but straightened up and got her cards ready. She flexed her fingers and shuffled the deck a few times. The entourage meandered down the street with members of the Japanese delegation talking to different 'street people'. Truthfully most of the people were no more street people than Red or Lizzy. The Underground wasn't the only group pulling strings on this day. Red worked hard at not looking eager. In fact she set her face in a sullen look. Trey had figured everyone else would be smiling and trying to catch the attention of the visitors. Someone who looked bored or unhappy would be almost sure to catch a visitor's eye. It was a matter of not going too far and scaring the security people.

About half way through the now winding line of the delegation, one of the Japanese came over to talk to her. He had a translator with him, but Red was certain he spoke better English than she did.

"Want to see a card trick, mister?" she asked, and held up the cards. She spread them out so the man could see all the cards in the deck were there. He looked bored already. "Heh, don't bother picking a card," she said, "I'll pick it for you." She fanned the deck face down and pushed it toward him. He hesitantly picked a card, but before he looked at it she said, "That's the red trey." He turned it over and looked puzzled.

"Red three, missy."

"S'what I said. Red trey. What we call the red three. It means something lost is found."

"Again." He handed the card back to Red and motioned for her to do it again. A crowd of Japanese delegates gathered around all talking at once in Japanese. She did the trick a half dozen times for different people. Each time she made sure to explain the red three was called the red trey. Finally D.C. Mulholland came over to find out what the holdup was. The whole crowd circled him and talked pointing at her.

"They are upset you call the three a trey. They are very particular about language."

"But you know about a red Trey, don't you?" He looked sharply at her. "What is lost can be found. Keep the card, sir. A reminder of today, maybe even a message of hope." D.C. Mulholland stared at her for a brief second then pocketed the card. Lizzy slipped Red another deck and she did her trick a few more times before security shepherded the delegates along. Red and Lizzy packed up and wandered away down the road. Once they were out of sight they made for the security perimeter and left the area after hearing they would not be allowed back in.

They walked briskly along until they came to a spot Trey was fairly certain would be on the path of the convoy on their way back to the negotiation tables. Red buzzed Trey they were in position. He replied he wasn't very far away.

The two lingered. It was almost evening when the convoy drove past. As they had hoped, it traveled slowly as the delegates headed to the embassy for the night. D.C. Mulholland's car was at the back of the convoy. They could see his head whip around when he saw them. He had the car stop, and he stormed over to them. The security people on their motorcycles were advancing in their direction.

"Trey needs to talk to you. It is now or never," Red said. She got up and walked into a coffee shop. Mulholland waved at the security people and pointed to the coffee shop. He flashed some hand sign to reassure them, and most of them returned to the convoy and continued on. One waited beside the car.

Red led Trey's father into the shop and walked to the end of the line. Instead of joining the queue, she walked through the back door to the waiting van. As she took the driver's seat, Trey opened the side door. His father climbed in followed by Lizzy and they merged into the city traffic.

***

The girls peeled off the small bits of silicone they had used to change the shape of their faces and deceive the face recognition software. Lizzy changed her coat and lost half a dozen years in the process. She left her wool cap on for the moment.

Mulholland had no time for either of the girls. He was staring at Trey, bereft of words. Trey knew Mulholland's face from the files, but the freckled skin and soft facial features looked more like him in person. The grey hair showed Trey his own future, should he live so long.

"So, do I pass muster, sir?" Trey asked.

"More than I had ever hoped, son," his father responded. "Your message was very clever. I doubt anyone will figure it out until it is too late. Having your lovely friends deliver it was a masterstroke."

"What am I?" As hard as Trey tried, as many times as he practiced that question, his voice still broke.

"Let me start with what you are not," Mulholland sighed and reached out toward Trey before pulling his hand back. "You are not a clone, a genetic enhancement, a monster, an organ bank, or anything else they might have told you. What you are is my son, but you are not just my son. Did you ever wonder who your mother was?"

The question opened a floodgate in Trey's mind. He'd never wondered about his mother. He'd suspected the woman he lived with was not his mother, but he had never questioned, even in his head who his real genetic mother was.

"What did you do to me?" He held his head to keep the thoughts from spilling out.

"Some gentle post-hypnotic suggestion. Ironically, intelligent people are more susceptible than others, not less. You were not to worry about your mother until I asked you about her.

"She was a loving and beautiful woman, but she also died close to a century before you were born. She had frozen her eggs in the hopes she would someday have children, but tragically died before she had the chance. I learned about the frozen ova, and decided the world needed her child, perhaps even more now, than when she had lived. I met her once and was smitten by her intelligence and grace, but I was already married and she was absorbed in her own life.

Besides I wasn't the kind of person she would have noticed. She was an iconoclast. Even then she was challenging the idea the old should rule the world. She prophesied horrible things if society didn't shift its attention to building up the young instead of subjugating them. She was right in just about every particular. She suggested a growing generation gap would almost completely sever the ties between ages and class in our country. Work would become virtual slavery to pay the bills for the old, and retirement would be a living hell for all but the very rich. The only thing she foresaw that hasn't happened yet is open conflict between the generations. And it is much closer than most people think."

Trey looked at Red and saw her nodding.

"I did everything I could to be sure you would inherit her brains, and you have. You look more like me than her." Mulholland shrugged. "Genetics. I don't know what they told you about me or about you. But that's all I can tell you here. I will tell you where to search for your mother, but be careful. Even after all this time they still monitor people who show too much interest in her."

"So, what do we do now?"

"We go back to what we were doing, for now. When it is safe I want to meet with you again and talk properly." Mulholland looked out the van window. "At least I know you are safe, and in good company. Watch Grant. He is the Methuselah who took you away from me. He and the people he works for are up to something, and whatever it is won't be good news for most of the people. He's ruthless and has been trying to use you to pressure me to support certain policies."

"Which ones?"

"They're an odd collection. One is the idea of changing the legal definition of identity to mind instead of body. Some countries have already gone that route, and are deep into quasi-legal research into rapid cloning. Another was to build up relations with countries with strong artificial organic programs. The last is an attempt to argue you achieve personhood at retirement, not birth. I can't see the last making any inroads except by a revolution. People might treat the young as slaves, but most still see them as people."

"You've been very helpful," Trey's mind threw patterns and possibilities together. "You might want to consider accepting an invitation to visit Japan."

"I haven't been...Do you think it's that close?"

"I can't be sure," Trey said, "but I would rather

not have to worry about you just now."

Red pulled the van over to the sidewalk.

"Here's a phone. You should be safe until your security gets here."

"Dad," Trey said as the door opened, "this is Red." He put a hand on her shoulder, "And Lizzy. They're friends."

"Thank you, son." Deputy Chancellor Mulholland shook Trey's hand, nodded at the girls and crossed the street. Red pulled away and made a number of random turns.

"We're clear," she said. "Are you alright?"

"I have my father back," he replied. "What do you think of him?"

"Seems like a nice guy." She shrugged. "He's your Dad." She caressed his cheek. "Let's go home."

Trey looked at the slip of paper his dad had slipped him. On it was the name of a woman who, just over a hundred years before, had been tried, convicted and executed for treason.

Back at the safe house, Trey rubbed Red's back while they talked. Lizzy was cooking up something for supper.

"From what my father said, I suspect a group in the Council is working on setting the groundwork for rule, not just by the rich and old, but by a small group of immortals. They're gambling either artificial biologicals or cloning and transplant technology will soon have a break-through which would let them live forever. They will share with no one. The only way they will be able to put all the 'reforms' into effect will be by open rebellion, or by imposing martial law. If they can force a rebellion by the Youngers they will be able to curtail the last few rights we have without any protest. Once they are in force, it won't be hard to manage them. A few people who are in the council will die; then they are effectively in complete control.

"It explains the policy shifts they are pressuring my father to approve. He's probably only one of many they are maneuvering. It also explains their manipulation of the Underground to exacerbate conditions. They want an armed rebellion, so they have an excuse to declare martial law. Even if we don't rebel, they'll manufacture an excuse, and impose restrictive laws anyway."

"So what do we do?" Asked Red. "If we do nothing, they win; if we do what we have trained to do they still win."

"I don't know yet," said Trey. "We need to talk to the Chief, and get word to the whole Underground, not just our section." He leaned forward to kiss Red on the forehead. "As much as I like being here with you, we need to go back to the Underground and talk to the others."

Lizzy brought a tray and set it on the table.

"OK, time to eat."

Trey looked at her and Lizzy shrugged.

"Red needs you to be happy." She set the plates on the table. "I'm not completely without feelings, but they're so much work I don't bother for people who aren't important. Easier to be a killing machine."

***

After lunch Red and Lizzy led Trey down into the tunnels and headed for the Underground. They took considerable time because they kept watch for dogbots and police patrols. They saw nothing but dog droppings and the occasional empty take-out coffee cup. They entered the Underground through a door he had never used before. Once inside the three made a direct line for the Chief's office.

Lizzy stopped at the door where she usually stood guard. "I will wait here."

Red shook her head. They walked along the familiar hallway and found Red's father staring at a map on the wall of his office.

"I've been waiting for you. I think we can get messages to all the underground groups quickly. All we need now is a message to send."

"I don't have any suggestions yet, sir." Trey's mind snapped back into working mode. "I'll have to do some research on possible responses which won't trigger exactly the situations they anticipate. If Red helps me, we can probably have some ideas within twenty-four hours. In the meantime, I have some suggestions for Jimmy and his team." He noticed Red and the Chief looking at him thoughtfully. "I'm angry with him, but I need his expertise."

"I'm furious," Red said. "But I can deal with it. What do you have in mind?"

"I am thinking we need to have an appropriate welcome when the Underground is invaded. I want to work up some strategies to create maximum chaos with minimum casualties." At Red's inquiring glance he explained further. "We need to live with these people, their families. They aren't the ones pulling the strings. That's the problem with civil war – you can't easily put the pieces back together. We don't want to split the country unless we have no other choice. We just want to bend it into a slightly different shape."

Red still looked doubtful, but the Chief was nodding his head.

"Our attack will be on the manipulators behind the scenes. We need to drag them into the light and let the people see them for what they are. So, what are you standing here for? Get to work." He made shooing motions and pushed the pair out of his office.

"Every time I think I know how your mind works, you surprise me again. I like that." She kissed him passionately. "Go find Annie and Bert. I'll meet you in the briefing room. I'll get Jimmy and bring him, in one piece, mostly." She pushed Trey away, then changed her mind and kissed him again.

Trey walked back to the briefing room trying to puzzle out this new relationship.

Annie and Bert were in the briefing room and greeted him as if he had been gone for lunch and not a couple of days. They put their heads together and began researching. History was full of revolutions and rebellions. The common factor seemed to be violence and carnage. In many countries cycles of rebellion and counter rebellion went on for generations. There was very little to hold out hope the geritocracy could be changed without bloodshed.

He closed the screen, then reopened it and typed in his mother's name. Information came up, contradictory, inflammatory, perhaps useful…

***

Trey was deep into his reading when Red entered with Jimmy. Dan and Lizzy followed.

"I thought we might as well have the whole team together," she said and deliberately sat next to

Trey. The others settled themselves around the table.

"I was looking at the Underground's possible responses to attack when I was unavoidably detained," Trey said, looking at the team. "Dogbots are effective for patrol topside, but they don't seem to like the tunnels. The evidence they left behind suggests they spent as much time trying to exit the tunnels as following orders. In the end they are only modified dogs. I don't think the local police were much more effective."

"I did research on police retirement." Red said. "No more than five percent of officers retire. I can imagine they would be concerned with their health."

"We can exploit that," Jimmy said, "and make it very dangerous for their health to come in here."

"We don't want to kill anybody." Trey looked at the pile of maps and plans as if he'd find a new answer.

"We can make it look dangerous. That would actually be better since we'd know it wasn't dangerous and be able to move freely."

"Add in some information about how unlikely it is they would survive anyway..." Red nodded and looked thoughtful. "We could have a lot of local police thinking there are better things to be doing than raiding the Underground."

"Especially if there's no one they can fight. I can't imagine anything thing worse than fighting your way through all kinds of dangers to discover there is no way to retaliate." Jimmy looked like his old self again.

"Jimmy, you and your team get to work on this.

Co-opt anyone you need to help. If you aren't sure about something run it past me, Trey or the Chief. Any more games, and the police will find you tied to a chair in the middle of the hall"

Jimmy fled the room.

"Dan," Red pointed at him, "you need to find alternate living space for everyone who hasn't moved out yet. I know some people don't want to leave, but find some place where they'll be comfortable for the interim. I don't want anyone arrested. The cops can't find anything but smoke and mirrors." Dan nodded and left.

"Annie and Bert, you're already working with Trey, but if you get a chance to talk about this to your friends, put a positive spin on it."

They nodded.

"Lizzy, the council will be moving out soon. The Chief has made arrangements. They won't be as comfortable, but they are secure. We have screened everyone who is involved in the planning and they are all clean. Communication out will also be screened and monitored. It is time we plugged the leaks. There are some folks who are going to be very upset. I would be happiest knowing you are watching the Council's back for the interim." Lizzy nodded and slipped out.

Red looked at Trey, and smiled. "Let's go for a walk."

Trey looked at Annie, and caught her nod. He smiled and took Red's hand.

"Sounds like a brilliant idea."

They walked through the tunnels, Red waving

and talking to everyone they met. They ended up at the café Dan had taken him to the first morning. The server brought them coffee and, between sips, they enjoyed the hustle and bustle of the market. Conversation floated around them. Trey added some of his coffee to lessen the sweetness of Red's. They held hands until both cups were cold.

"I'll miss this," Red said. "Whether we win or lose, this will be gone."

"This is community, the way it should be. If we win there will be more of this, everywhere."

"So you'd better make sure we win, Trey."

"I'm doing my best, Red."

***

Shortly, they were back in the briefing room. Red ran a few computer searches.

"There is nothing new, no report D.C. Mulholland wandered away for an hour. No new announcements from Molloy. There's never been much on Grant." She looked at Trey. "I don't know if that is a good thing or not."

"Can you search social trends?" asked Trey. "I would like to see what people are thinking about freedom and responsibility. How many people are saving for retirement or if they are saving. Have they given up hope of a better life?"

Red looked thoughtful for a moment then started typing away.

"Your best bet isn't the polls, it is the blogs. People put everything in their blogs. I can send out a search bot looking for the parameters you mentioned." She finished typing. " Now we just wait.

You know what? Your dad didn't tell you the name of your mother."

"He did," said Trey, handing her the slip of paper.

She opened it up. "Oh...." It was the first time he had ever seen her lost for words.

After a while she came over and sat on his knee and hugged him long and hard. She looked at him.

"Are you alright?"

"As long as you are here."

"You always say the finest things," Red said, kissing him between each word.

"I have the message to go out to the other Undergrounds. My mother taught me what to do."

***

Jimmy worked harder than ever before. The watchful eyes of his security commander never left him. One stupid joke and they thought he was a traitor. He had spray-painted the walls with invisible graffiti, nursing his resentment. After all he'd helped rescue Trey. You'd think they'd trust him now.

He moved to a different part of the mall and his shadow moved too.

"Hey, kid," the commander came over to him. "We're done here. Go back to your room and wait for orders."

"What, you still think I'm a traitor?"

"Nobody thinks you're a traitor," his commander said. "We think you're an idiot." He pushed Jimmy toward his room.

Jimmy walked with his head swirling. He almost missed his room.

His escort shoved him through the door and closed it.

Jimmy sat on the bed staring at the wall as his commander's words echoed in his head.

HOSTAGE

Devon handed Joe a coffee. The events of the day seemed to dictate the need for a second break. First - the picture of Molloy at the burned out house hadn't been downloaded or forwarded. The really interesting thing was the girl hadn't taken the picture; it had been uploaded to the phone and was actually a very good fake. Devon found a phone number embedded in the picture. The assumption they would find it was a backhanded compliment.

They filed the number and had barely begun discussing those implications when Devon's search bots picked up a security call - D.C. Mulholland had apparently gone missing for almost an hour. He returned none the worse for wear, but refused to say where he had gone. The younger security people thought he had made an arrangement with a couple of girls he had met on a walkabout shortly before. The older ones weren't so sure, but they weren't talking.

As part of Mulholland's brief disappearance the

pictures of a few girls was circulated. There was no trace of their identity or of their existence. The security people shrugged it off. A lot of street people didn't exist in the system. Devon happened to notice a wisp of hair sticking out from under a wool cap. The same blue they had seen from the jailbreak video. For some reason the resistance was talking to Mulholland. It had to be a friendly talk since the Deputy Chancellor had been found unscathed just a short distance away.

The piece of information, which prompted the coffee break, was the news Chancellor O'Brien was sending his Deputy to Japan in order to continue negotiations and demonstrate this country was willing to learn from other peoples and cultures. As part of his duties, he was now Trade Consul to Japan, which, while not a step up in the hierarchy, was a better title than Deputy Chancellor. He would leave next week.

"Someone is clearing the table for action." Joe picked up his cup and cradled it in his hands. "Since Grant would keep his players close at hand, Trey must have given him a message during their meeting."

"Trey's involvement with the resistance makes sense. It explains the way he disappeared the first time and the rescue from the jail. It also explained the look on Trey's face when Grant questioned him. Trey expected to be questioned about his resistance activities, not about his father. Grant's questions prodded the young man to find a way to talk to his father." Devon sipped at the coffee and grimaced. It had gone cold.

Joe finished his coffee and sighed.

"There are two reasons Grant might have been asking the wrong questions. One is he is completely unaware of the resistance and focused only on Trey; the other is he already believes he knows whatever he needs and therefore didn't ask more questions. There's no two ways about it, Devon. We need to get in touch with the resistance. I am missing pieces they have. I'm sure I know things they don't. Can we use the number on a secure line to contact them?"

"We can use the number, but it will be recorded as an outgoing call, even on a secure line. You might want to think low tech."

"A burner phone."

"Right. The numbers can be downloaded, but only if they get hold of the phone you used. You just need to be very thorough in the destruction of the phone"

"I think I know where to meet. It is private and they will feel safe. If I don't come back, do what you think is best with my files."

"You are going now?"

"There's no time like the present. I have a feeling things are coming to a head." Joe picked up his cane and headed for the door. "One more thing." He walked back to his desk, and pulled up a map. "I would like you to unlock and cancel the security on this one door. I may need a back door to get back in."

Devon took the coffee cups to the little kitchen to wash and put them away. Back at the desk he sent a brief message. Within seconds of sending the message, every trace it had ever existed had been erased. Devon stretched and sighed. There was work to do before Joe got back.

***

Joe made his way out onto the street and wandered through the afternoon crowd. Most were Youngers dashing everywhere in their eternal quest for future security. There were a couple of retirees, who walked slower, not just from age, but from the assurance they had arrived and no longer needed to hurry anywhere. Joe came to a corner store and figured it was as good as any. He bought a phone for cash then dialed the number.

"Hello?"

"Hello," Joe said. "I would like to talk to someone about a young man named Trey Gauche."

"And why do you think I know such a person?"

"Because if you did not you would have just told me I dialed a wrong number. I suggest we meet at the underpass where he vanished."

"There are a lot of underpasses."

"I think Trey will know the one I'm thinking of. I'll wait until sundown." Joe hung up and flagged a taxi. He had the driver leave him close by the underpass and walked the rest of the way. The light was dim, but he could see the graffiti; some of it looked worn enough to have come from his own teenaged days. He set himself comfortably against the wall and waited.

The sun had almost set, when figures entered the underpass from each end. At one end Joe could see a silhouette of tall man, at the other a shorter man carrying a stick. He tightened his grip on his cane and waited for them to get to him. Before they arrived an access cover shifted in front of him and a youngster with blue hair climbed out. She was followed by another young woman, who looked at him suspiciously.

"Leave your cane against the wall," she ordered. "Jimmy brought one for you without the implements of torture embedded in it." Joe did as he was told. The blue-haired child raised his cane and examined it speculatively. If the lab was right she was over fifty, but she looked ten at the most.

"Let's go," the second girl waved at the access tunnel. "Do you need help?"

"I think I can manage," Joe replied. "The control for the cane is on the brass ring. It is biometrically matched to me, so others can't use it, but I don't know what would happen if you try to break into it."

The blue haired Younger shrugged, and handed the cane to the shorter man. Joe took a deep breath and climbed down the ladder. There were two more young people at the bottom waiting for him. The others followed him down. The tall man closed the access cover. They surrounded him, staring suspiciously.

"You called because you think you have information I need," a voice behind him said. Joe turned. Trey walked up the tunnel carrying a folding chair. When he arrived he set it up and waved Joe into it.

"I definitely have information you need." The

other two men faded back into the darkness, leaving Joe with Trey and the girls.

"My name is Joe. I'm a Methuselah, as you have obviously guessed. I did come to exchange information, but also because I think we need each other. There appears to be conspiracy at the highest levels to give a handful of would-be immortals complete control. The man who tortured you is working for them. He's also the one trying to pressure your father, and others, to comply with their 'reforms'. Since he has access to all the criminal case files, included blocked files, he is likely the one who was manipulating your group into removing certain people so he could put his own people in place."

"And what do you want, Joe?" Trey asked.

"I want what I have wanted for more than a century - justice. I want to live in a society which treats everyone as human beings."

"Pretty words, but how can we trust you?" the girl asked belligerently.

"I have put myself into your hands," Joe said. "Either you will listen or you won't, but there isn't much time. Things are coming to a head, and somebody is going to have to act fast to stop them."

"You're talking about armed revolt," Trey said.

"Only as a last resort," Joe replied. "There must be some on the Council who aren't in on the plot, or the inner group wouldn't need to be so secretive."

"But how many would turn down the chance to live forever, if it were offered to them?" Trey leaned against the wall and glowered at him.

"Not everyone wants to live forever. Some of us

are content to live the days we are given, but we all need to answer for ourselves. In the meantime we need to prevent a small group from stealing life from the young to sustain themselves."

"Why would you care?" Red stood in front of him with hands on her hips. "You can quit tomorrow and live comfortably for the rest of your life."

"My wife and son were killed while I saved the life of man who then perverted everything I believed in. I have spent the rest of my life atoning for my mistake. I don't expect you to believe me or welcome me with open arms, but I do think you should listen to what I have to say."

"Fair enough. You have told us all the problems are the fault of a conspiracy in the Council. What do you plan to do about it?" If anything, Red's stance became more hostile.

"Actually the problems are the result of human greed and short-sightedness. The conspiracy has just used existing problems to further their own agenda. I think the fundamental issue is we have put the burden of supporting the retirees on the shoulders of the young. But our immediate problem is to create a response to the threat posed by the Council plot. I believe they are led by Councilor Molloy."

"I killed him. He didn't want to die, but he did," the blue haired child spoke from behind him.

Joe set aside his astonishment. She was their executioner?...though it made a horrible kind of sense.

"You executed a biological construct which may or may not have had Molloy's organic brain. I suspect it didn't, because the crimes he committed were not the kind that the Molloy I knew would do. I suspect he knew his double was raping and killing children and he manipulated you into killing it to save him the embarrassment of having his own people do it."

"So you figure the double was trying to find a way to have relationships, but didn't have the tools to relate in a healthy way?" Trey asked.

"If he was Molloy's double he wouldn't have the means. I never met anyone who cared less about other people. It's easy to believe he would destroy our country to guarantee himself a comfortable immortality. He wouldn't see any drawbacks. He's been using a Methuselah named Grant to do his dirty work. Trey, at least, has met him a couple of times."

"So he would send in armed troops led by Grant to kill everyone in the Underground to change the laws to his advantage." Trey's hand twitched slightly as he frowned at Joe.

"Underground, right. I had been calling you the resistance myself. But yes he would, and he will, as soon as you give him the excuse he needs. So you need to have your response ready. I hate the idea of civil war, but what Molloy is doing is worse. I should have let him die way back when, but I refused to admit what kind of man he was."

"All right," Red stepped away from him. "Our source said he could be trusted if any of them could. She beamed a smile at him completely changing her from threatening to receptive. "You aren't the only ones with spies." Her eyes sparkled in a way suggesting she knew something of vital importance he didn't. No time to worry about it now.

"We aren't going to fight," Trey said. "We don't have the people or the weapons to have any impact on the local police, never mind the army. Besides, they want a war, bloodshed and chaos, because it will cover their actions until it is too late. They'll blame the troublesome youth. We are going to try it my mother's way."

"Your mother? There is no mother's name associated with you, just your father. That's why Molloy thinks you are some kind of clone."

"Not a clone, a test tube baby. My mother died more than a century ago. Her name was Aneeta Ghandi. She was executed for treason - for organizing a riot against the changes the government enacting."

"The charges were bogus. She was exercising her right to free speech. The treason charge, the connection to terror groups was all fabricated." Joe rubbed his eyes. After all these years, it still hurt.

"You knew her?" Trey moved away from the wall to crouch down in front of Joe.

"You have her eyes. The rest of you is all Mulholland, but you have her eyes." Joe shook his head. "I had evidence to prove she was being set up, but she forbade me to present it. She thought they would have destroyed me along with her. She was probably right. Another thing for me to atone for, letting her die."

"It sounds like you have a lot to atone for," Red said.

"When you have lived for more than two hundred years, you do."

"So why aren't you on the council?"

"I didn't want to get involved in the politics."

"Something else for you to regret," Lizzy spoke up for the first time.

"Let's stop Molloy, and I will do what I can," Joe said. "Now, how do you plan to respond?"

"By not doing anything."

"How is that going to stop them?"

"When my mother was arrested she was advocating a general strike. It never happened because they got to her first. We are going to make it work. The word has already gone out through the Underground. At the signal, they stop work and go home. There is to be no violence, no protests. As the government increases the pressure, others will follow suit. We can shut down the country. It should distract them long enough for us to get to the other part of the plan."

"The other part?"

"Yes, shutting down the country will still give them the excuse to impose martial law. So we will need to take control of the council until we can negotiate reform."

"I think I can help you with that part."

TO LIVE FOREVER

Grant knocked on the door near the top floor of the Justice building. He put his thumb on the biometric lock with the usual twinge of fear. If he didn't clear, the lock would send enough electricity through him to kill him on the spot. Grant didn't like the idea of dying. The door opened and he walked through one room and into the next. He'd stopped noticing the crude appearance of the room. All he cared about was the thin figure attached to countless wires and tubes reclining on the bed.

"I see things are coming to a head." Councilor Molloy walked in through the other door.

"The boy doesn't know anything about his father's plans. He appears very healthy for a clone if he is one."

"Mulholland must have a reason for having the boy made."

"Not everything is about immortality."

"Wrong, immortality is everything. Mulholland is hiding his light. He is far smarter than he looks." Molloy thumped the wall. "He may have found an answer while I decay slowly. I need the boy. He has the answers. I am not pleased you may have damaged him. Worse, you let him loose."

"I put a locator in him. I can pick him up anytime I want to."

"Pick him up. Now."

"Yes, sir, and the other part of the plan?" Grant said.

"Strike when you are ready. I want the country so terrified they will beg me to take control. They will give me their putrid children just so they can have their precious hope of retirement."

"And then?"

"You will have what you want, Grant. Years to enjoy your life without the inconvenient restrictions the young put on us."

"Are the copies becoming more stable?"

"No, you fool, instead of years of slow decline, our minds collapse in weeks."

Grant nodded and turned to leave.

"The boy, Grant, the boy is the key. My people will be able to take him apart and learn how to make me young again."

Grant closed the door behind him. He wasn't sure about Molloy. He didn't like fanatics, but the old man was useful for now. Grant took the elevator down to his office. He refused to work in a basement like Joe. He wanted the recognition due him. He signed on to the computer and checked the status of the people he had marked for elimination. There had been no more executions. The artificial Molloy had been the last. It was as if they had gotten scared when they met something they couldn't understand. Their fear was weakness. Time to make them crack. They would be the destruction of the very thing they were trying to preserve. The plan needed just one more push.

He checked to see if there were any flags on the other names he was watching. D.C. Mulholland's name came up twice. Grant knew about him ducking away from the delegation for almost an hour with no explanation. The speculation ran from the pornographic to the mundane. Grant was sure Mulholland had made contact with Trey.

Shortly after, D.C. Mulholland had been appointed Consul to Japan and dispatched there to 'build strong trade relationships'. He'd just flown out.

What was so important he would take the risk now? Why leave the country and not take Trey with him? He thought the boy was safe from Grant's people. Grant picked up the phone to order Trey arrested at the last location of the tracker.

Then another flag caught his attention. Joe was gone from his office. He was last seen the day after Mulholland met with Trey, buying a cell phone. The number couldn't be traced, but Grant didn't need it. He pulled up the recording from the people he had tailing Joe. Soon, he found what he was seeking. The old fool had set up a meeting with the resistance. They wouldn't be anywhere near the meeting site. It didn't matter. Why chase ants when he could destroy the nest?

There was a Methuselah being held by an armed resistance. It was Grant's duty to rescue him, whether he wanted it or not. With any luck, he'd already be dead.

He picked up the phone and dialed the City Police.

"Connect me to the Chief of Police," Grant said, "I have a priority one emergency."

When the Chief came on the line Grant snapped his orders.

"A terrorist group has taken a Methuselah hostage. I am sending you a tape and the address now. These people are armed and dangerous. Take no chances. I want them shut down immediately. My sources have mapped out their location. I'm sending you the file now. Send patrols and use extreme caution. Yes, I believe these are the same terrorists involved in the vicious jail break." He cut the connection.

The Police Chief would lead his people into a trap. He'd learned that much before communication broke down. When they were cut to pieces, he'd send in the army. They'd stamp out a few riots, and declare martial law. Finally, Grant would have the tools to control the country.

He leaned back. It was satisfactory to finally deal with these fanatics. When Joe had brought up the possibility of a Youngers' resistance, he had immediately recognized their usefulness. Councilor Molloy had agreed. It wasn't advantageous to be immortal without having free rein.

He buzzed his assistant. "Bring me coffee." He might as well be comfortable while he waited. Grant pulled up the feed from the City Police. He would relish this.

****

The SWAT team smashed the door in and poured into the apartment. Within seconds they determined it was empty. They did unearth a dirty and well folded map of the tunnels beneath the city, though it had objects marked on it no city map included, much more detailed than the vague sketches he'd been sent. The Chief of Police allowed himself a patronizing smile. The Methuselah was waiting to hand out little snippets of information. It was time to show him what the well-trained city force could accomplish. In minutes he had mobilized the entire department and sent them to break into the burrow these traitorous rats had mined for themselves. He even geared up and went to enjoy the action.

Common Cause

While Trey, Red and Lizzy took Joe to a different safe house, Dan led the others back to the Underground.

The Underground mall was dim and quiet. Only a few dozen people remained working feverishly to install the last of their surprises for the expected invaders. The Middlers' council had cut all communication with the outside. As each part was completed another squad would make its way to the surface and split up across the city. They were given the task of starting a whisper campaign to lay the groundwork for the strike. What better way to fight back against those who exploited their labor than to go home and deprive the leaders of the value of their work?

Finally, only Jimmy was left with Annie, Bert and Dan.

"It seems strange," Annie said. "I've never seen it this empty before. It feels like we are giving up."

"We need to trust Trey," Dan said. "The word about the general strike is spreading fast. Our folks top-side say the public is balanced on a knife edge.

We're primed and ready. We don't need the Underground anymore."

"Yeah, here's hoping," Jimmy led the way to the massive entrance from the market to the tunnels. "After you." He watched the other three walk through the door, then pushed a button on the remote in his pocket. The door clanged shut locking him in. "Sorry guys," Jimmy's voice came through the hidden speaker by the door. "Someone needs to run the show."

Dan banged on the door for ten minutes before Annie and Bert dragged him away.

"He's made his decision. We need to get into position," Bert said.

"We don't need any heroes." Dan shook his head. "We'll need him to get into the Council."

"Trey will find a way."

"Just so long as Jimmy's alive at the end of all this."

The three walked down the tunnel toward the rendezvous point.

***

A large steel door disguised with concrete blocked access from the tunnel into a large open space Police teams coordinated their attacks to start when it was blown. For all its size and weight the engineered explosives demolished it in seconds. Dust and gravel filled the area. No one noticed the tiny video camera. The SWAT team poured through the door, burdened with all their equipment. Immediately the space they were in went black as the power was cut. The squad flipped their night vision goggles into position and began working their way into the maze of paths and booths filling the cavernous space. They had penetrated about twenty-five yards when the strobe lights came on.

Officer D'Aoust's goggles didn't work quite quickly enough and the lights blinded him. He tore them off his face while others around him flipped theirs up. His squad leader tried to send him back, but D'Aoust wasn't going to let a few spots prevent him from being front and center in the biggest bust of his career. He blinked the pain away and moved to the next position. The strobes flashed at irregular intervals making coordination difficult, but they managed. Something interfered with their radios, so they had to resort to shouting. Other groups faced similar problems. His squad started shooting out the strobes. Darkness was easier to handle. Soon they put the goggles back on.

D'Aoust no longer trusted his night vision goggles so he used his flashlight. The squad leader got him to signal their status back down the line. Communications found a channel which wasn't jammed.

Then the music started.

D'Aoust was a music fan, but this was louder than any concert he'd ever attended. It drowned out everything until they could put earplugs in place. Even through the earplugs he could hear the demented march playing. Along with the music, the lights started coming on and off. Not as bad as the strobes, but difficult nevertheless.

They started kicking in doors and checking

rooms.

No one. All the disruption with the lights and sound appeared to be automated. Then the door D'Aoust's partner kicked in activated a smoke grenade. The stench was enough to make them sick, even after they repositioned their gas masks. They continued demolishing doors and finding no people, but plenty of trouble. One team was gassed by something which made every bit of exposed skin itch. Buckets balanced on doors soaked some. They growled and continued the search.

D'Aoust congratulated himself on at least being dry when the sprinklers came on. They got rid of the smoke pretty quick, but every strap on his gear started chafing at him. He desperately wanted to shoot someone. It was one huge practical joke. He hated practical jokes.

He came to one more door among the hundreds and broke it down. But instead of another empty room or a smoke bomb there was a punk at a computer. The kid was laughing as he turned to face the officer. He put his hands up, but somehow, D'Aoust's finger tightened on the trigger anyway. The shot took the young man high in the chest. He looked more disappointed than angry. As he slid to the floor he punched one more key. All the lights went out then ultraviolet lights came on. All over the walls words glowed.

Only five percent of you will survive to retire.
You could all be dead.
Is it worth it?
D'Aoust holstered his gun and yelled for a

medic. The kid was bleeding badly; the blood black under the ultraviolet light. The officer worked to quell the bleeding but managed only to slow the flow. D'Aoust heard the medics coming.

"Hold on, kid. You aren't going to die on me." His tears burned worse than the gas. Wrenching sobs fought past his control.

"So they made you a killer," whispered the kid. "Is it worth it?" He closed his eyes and let his head fall back.

The medics took over from D'Aoust, but shook their heads.

D'Aoust's heart ached. He'd signed up to protect people, not to shoot unarmed kids. He headed out of the complex.

The Police Chief interrupted a general command to the force to stop him.

"What are you doing? We've work to do."

"It's just children playing games," D'Aoust said. "There are no dangerous rebels here."

"You don't know that."

"Yeah, I do." He dropped his badge and gun on the floor. "I'm quitting. It isn't worth it."

He walked away and the Police Chief went back to his announcement to realize he'd broadcast the entire dialogue to the whole force. He swore then threatened dire punishment to any who deserted.

Most of the officers continued to scramble through the dark, checking rooms and hollering to each other. Unnoticed in the chaos, others also abandoned their weapons and badges to follow D'Aoust.

***

The Chief sat with the Underground Council and followed the chaos of the police attack through the monitors Jimmy patched through to them. They witnessed his shooting and the police officer's tears as he cradled his victim. They heard Jimmy's last words. Somberly, they moved to the next stage. Jimmy was the first, but he wouldn't be the last to die. They sent the signal out to their people across the city, and to the other Underground factions in other cities.

All across the nation people stopped working and went home. Some of them explained their actions, others didn't. Production lines shut down; grocery stores were short of cashiers, deliveries halted. Word spread swiftly. Some who were left became frustrated and they too headed home.

A video began circulating from cell phone to cell phone. It showed a police officer kicking in a door then shooting an unarmed teen. It showed the cop weeping then screaming for the medics. Then it played a dialogue between the officer and the Police Chief. It finished with a message.

Is it worth it? Go home.

More people abandoned their posts. Supervisors struggled to stop the flow, but were ignored or pushed aside. In one factory the management locked the exits. They tried to force workers to return to their stations. Skirmishes broke out between workers and security. One of the men was caught in a machine and crushed to death. A security guard hit the emergency stop then opened the doors. Everyone disappeared, leaving the factory silent and empty.

The trickle became a flood. More and more businesses and industries were abandoned. Managers shrugged their shoulder and followed the employees. Phones sent messages back and forth. Videos showed empty aisles in stores, silent machines in factories. Always the question, 'Is it worth it?'

The police left the Underground, disillusioned. The terrible enemy was a kid playing jokes. They watched the body being loaded into the coroner's van and more of them walked away. In the streets around them people moved quietly toward their homes. The flood swallowed the police officers and carried on.

Grant put a Molloy simulation on the television to ask people to return to work. Their protest had been heard. It was time for calmer heads to prevail. A work stoppage of this magnitude could do permanent damage to the economy.

The broadcast hadn't finished when a video of Grant torturing a young man in a jail cell started making the rounds. More people left their work and went home.

***

In a Sunnydale Home, the Younger staff walked off the job, while the administrator raged and hurled insults. *Ungrateful wretches, the whole lot of them.* She had a business to run and they whined about dignity and respect.

The dining room was full of elders in wheelchairs or walkers. Not one of them was independent or could care for themselves in any way. They sat there

236

destroying her profitability. Let them starve. She loathed them for their weakness. Moans instead of words, drooling, shaking. But she needed them. They were her ticket away from a place just like this. If she could make just a bit more profit per resident...

The administrator went to her office and began running numbers. There had to be some way out of this. It wasn't her fault. Presently she heard sounds from the dining room - laughter, conversation. Curious, she went to investigate. The staff was feeding the elders.

"You know you aren't supposed to be taking so much time feeding them." She tapped her watch.

"We aren't here for you." A nurse glared at her, looked around the room. "We're here for them. We'll take care of things. You go back to your office."

"What am I supposed to do there?"

"Well, you are getting close to retirement. You could be praying you don't end up in a Home run by someone like you." The nurse went back to feeding an old woman whose hands shook uncontrollably.

***

Grant ground his teeth in frustration. There was no bloodshed, no fighting, except isolated pockets where managers had tried a little too diligently to keep their workforce at the job. The entire raid on the Underground had been a shambles, the only casualty some snot-nosed punk. He needed some action, some strife, some excuse. He made a call to a General.

"No sir. I can't send the army out just because people are going home," the General said. "It doesn't matter if you order it. I'll be the one with blood on my hands."

"I'm ordering you to restore order."

"I know, but I can't restore order if there is no disorder."

Grant slammed the phone down in its cradle. Then he dialed the commander of the army base outside of town.

"Put your people on alert, Colonel. There's trouble coming."

He thought for a moment then called the power company.

"What is your status?" he asked. "How long will you be able to hold out?" Grant smiled and called the Colonel back.

"Get your people to the power station. I want them kept up and running at any cost. We can't afford to have the city lose power."

He sat back and watched the monitors, waiting for the bloodbath to begin.

***

The Colonel was a hard-nosed commander who took his job seriously, but he was taken aback when the convoy arrived at the generating plant to discover no unrest, no riots, just people refusing to work. But he had been given orders, so he set a cordon across the gate to block the workers' exit.

"Back to work," he shouted through the bullhorn. "It is essential we continue to have power."

The men and women just stared at him and refused to move.

"I have been given direct orders by the highest

authority to keep this power plant open and running."

"So what?" one of the men asked. "If you want it running, run it yourself. I am going home." He began walking toward the cordon of army personnel. The rest followed him.

The Colonel ordered his people to ready their weapons, but the crowd kept coming.

"If you shoot me, who is going to do my job?" a woman asked. "Are you able to replace me?"

The front line of the army squadron wavered.

"Shoot the next person who moves," the Colonel screamed.

The first man to speak was face to face with a private whose shaking hands barely could hold his rifle.

"Either shoot me, or get out of my way."

"Shoot him, soldier," the sergeant yelled.

"I can't, he isn't armed."

"You were given an order soldier! Are you refusing an order?"

"Yes, I guess I am."

The sergeant pointed his weapon at the private.

"Shoot him, or I will shoot you."

The young private put his gun on the ground and faced the sergeant.

"I didn't sign up to shoot unarmed civilians. Did you?"

The sergeant held his raised weapon for a long second then lowered it.

"No, son, I didn't." All down the line weapons lowered. The cordon stepped back and allowed the power station personnel to leave.

The Colonel ranted at his subordinates, to no avail. He pulled his sidearm and put it to the head of the private.

"Pick up your gun, soldier." He waited a second. "I won't tell you again. Pick up your gun." Frustrated beyond belief, he pulled the trigger. Nothing happened. The sergeant took the gun. Two other non-coms seized his arms.

"It works better if you take off the safety, Sir." The 'Sir' as insulting as a sergeant could make it. The sergeant looked at a young lieutenant. "Orders?"

"Well, arrest him, for attempted murder." The lieutenant pointed at the Colonel. "Let's go home, folks, and leave these people in peace." His army cheered and they returned to the vehicles. The Colonel sat ignored between two sergeants, muttering and cursing.

An hour later when the power station shut down, it knocked out the entire eastern grid.

***

Grant threw his phone across the room. All his work and nobody wanted to fight. Was everyone a coward? He had tried declaring martial law, but the weary voice at the other end of the line had told him most of the soldiers had gone AWOL.

"Well, gather what's left and do something," Grant shouted. "We'll bring people in from other bases."

"There are no other people," the General said. "It's all across the country. Nobody wants to die for a bunch of old people who don't care anyway."

"I'll have you court-martialed!"

"You and what army? Take this as my early retirement. I'm going to the officer's mess and getting drunk."

Grant stared at the phone in his hand then hung up. He just didn't understand.

His door opened and four people carrying flashlights walked into his office.

DEATH WALKS
AMONG US.

Joe walked up to the Justice Building and propped himself against the wall. Trey paced while Red and Lizzy leaned on either side of him.

"Be patient," Joe said quietly, "my secretary will open the door when it's clear."

Joe and his companions had waited for almost half an hour before it opened.

"Follow me," Devon instructed them. He led them up the stairs to Joe's office. Devon brought in extra chairs for the visitors, then brought in coffee and served it. They sat in silence as they sipped. This time it was Devon who broke the silence.

"Well, Charlene, you have grown."

"Oh Mom, you know I want to be called Red."

"I know, I know," Devon sighed. "But a mother has a problem seeing her daughter so grown up."

"I'm guessing here," Joe said, "but there must be a lot of things you aren't telling me."

"It's a long story, Joe," she said.

"It isn't like we don't have time," he replied.

"Oh, alright. But I warn you it is almost as boring as it is long." Devon took a sip of her coffee. "I married Charlene's father a number of years ago. We hit it off and were doing well in life. Charlene, I mean Red." She sighed and nodded at her daughter. "It was the happiest time of my life. We were living a life most people just dream about. Then disaster struck. My contract was cancelled. I couldn't find another job at the same level and I ended up as a clerk again. Then he lost his legs in an accident at work. With money being tight, our relationship suffered.

"Your father, Red, couldn't let go of the unfairness. Our lives had been ruined to make some other person's life more comfortable. Finally we separated to spare you our constant bickering. He took you and vanished. For years all I would get was the occasional letter with a photo of an ever more beautiful daughter. I scraped my way back up the heap playing by the rules, while you and your father risked everything to change those rules.

"Maggie told me this position as secretary was available, but you, Joe, would probably be more open to someone older than me. I got to know her when we were testing software for Justice. We decided I should become Devon and 'age' a few years. I have enjoyed myself more here as Joe's secretary than at any other job I have ever had." Devon glanced at Joe. "The only thing that rankled was I had to lie to you every day, but that was the only lie. In every other way I gave you only myself. When we started unraveling the nature of the plot in the Council I knew it was time I threw my efforts into the struggle for a better world for my daughter.

"It was easy to call the number I'd traced and get in touch with Red's father. I called him to let him know you were coming, Joe, to the meeting and I thought you could be trusted."

"That explains Red looking like she was in on some bizarre joke." Joe inclined his head to her. "I'm sure your references made my work a lot easier, Devon."

"Then I waited for you to come back." Devon wiped her eyes. "I hoped I would get a chance to see my daughter again. So here she is changing the world." She got up and hugged Red. "How's your father?"

"Doing great, missing you every day."

"When all this is done maybe we can work something out."

"Mom, just lose the man thing first. You might freak him out."

"Don't worry," Devon laughed. "Your father's seen me in a suit before. Even in this day and age people don't believe women can write security software. He's used to me looking rather masculine. I just never expected to take it this far."

"Ok, you'll freak me out." Red shook herself. "Mom, this is Trey." She took his hand. "I think you know who he is and all, but I need to introduce him to you, not his file."

Devon reached over and took Trey's hand. "I feel privileged to meet you, Trey. I'm impressed at the quick response to the strike call."

"The general strike picks up on the feeling of helplessness. They can't change anything, but they can go home. In the short term, going home won't even make their situation worse. We had whisper campaigns going on and planted some ideas in the most popular blogs. All of them are supporting us. Even ex-military bloggers were hinting at illegal orders and the need for soldiers to stand up for the country by refusing the wrong kind of commands." Trey grinned wryly. "The Council did a lot of the work for us by so thoroughly isolating the young. People were ready to act, and not inclined to heed the Council."

Suddenly, the lights failed and didn't come back on.

"What happened to the emergency generator?" Joe asked.

"Somebody turned it off. I also sent out the video of Grant and Trey to counteract Molloy's appeal for people to return to work while the Council resolved the issues."

"I knew there was a reason I liked you. I mean besides the coffee. If I'm lucky, I'll get to meet your husband." Joe pushed himself to his feet. "Let's go. Devon, you're in charge here. Make sure the momentum continues to build. I'm sure you can find other tidbits to broadcast but keep the anger from escalating. We want people safe in their homes, not rampaging on the streets.

"Subtle. I got you." Devon smiled and handed flashlights to them.

"It might also be useful if you can isolate Grant while we deal with him. Lock the security people down as much as you can. It may not stop them, but it will give us time."

Joe turned and led the way to the stairs. Trey, Red and Lizzy followed him.

"Your Mom's pretty cool," Trey whispered. Red squeezed his hand.

They arrived at the fourth floor and took a moment to catch their breath. Joe had paused at a door midway down the corridor.

"This is it." Joe opened the door, and they walked in taking up positions on either side of the door.

"Well, Grant. I am not sure this is what you had in mind, but I am impressed." Joe sounded as if he had just bumped into Grant in the elevator.

"I should have known you were mixed up in this," the other Methuselah said. "You always had a soft spot for any Younger with a sob story. When I've mopped this up, you'll be up for treason." Grant pushed a button on his board. "Forces loyal to the Council are on their way.

"You were a Younger once."

"I grew out of it. You should try it. The world is for the strong. Take what you need, or someone else takes it. I got tired of waiting for my turn."

"You want to live forever."

"Damned right I do. I worked hard to get where I am."

"Old and miserable. You will just get older and more miserable every day. Immortality won't change that."

"You're a fool. Life isn't about being happy. It is

about being strong."

"It isn't about either of them."

"Right, the all wise Joe is going to tell me about life." Grant pushed the button again.

"Hardly, and you wouldn't listen anyway."

"We aren't done yet." Grant lifted his cane and stabbed it at Joe. Joe narrowly avoided it.

"You haven't forgotten your cane, have you?" Grant jabbed again, and again missed by a whisker. He laughed. "I will enjoy watching you die."

Lizzy moved in from his right. Grant swung the cane up and activated it. Lizzy had drawn her knives. She couldn't reach to stab Grant, but the blades made contact with the skin over his heart. Twenty thousand volts traveled through the woman in the child's body, through her knives and into Grant's heart. He tried to scream, but the jolt stifled it. He couldn't release the cane, and Lizzy couldn't move the knives. Grant's heart gave out and he dropped to the floor. The cane clattered down beside him. Lizzy hung on to her knives and with iron will returned them to her sheathes.

"That hurt," she said.

"You're stronger than you look," Joe nudged the cane with his foot. "Not many people would still be standing." He bent down and picked up the cane. "Might come in useful."

"Now what?" Red asked.

"I think it is time to pay a visit to the Council," Joe replied.

"We don't know who was involved," Trey said.

"I don't think it matters. They are all

accountable." Joe offered his hand to Lizzy. "If you would allow me to help..."

Lizzy took his arm and they walked out of the room. Red glanced and Trey. They both shrugged and then followed.

Joe led them back to the stairs.

"We are heading for the top floor. Are you OK?"

"OK," Lizzy said.

Joe nodded and they started up the stairs. Two floors from the top they came up to an old woman resting on the steps. She leaned on her cane and breathed deeply.

"I found the most disturbing information today," she said. "I don't know how I missed it he first time I went through the files." She aimed her cane at Joe. Lizzy stepped in front of him. "Don't worry, dear. I took the battery out years ago. I could never stand the thought of zapping someone."

"So what are you doing here, Roberta?" Joe asked.

"The elevator isn't working. I need to ask Council a few questions."

"You were going to just walk in to the Council chambers and ask questions?" said Red.

"Why not?"

"I knew there was a reason I sent you those files," Joe said.

Trey offered his arm to the Methuselah. She clutched it and heaved herself up.

"Let's go." The five of them climbed up the last few flights and came out in a richly appointed hallway. There was light in this hallway. Two towering guards guarded the massive double doors far down the corridor. They glowered at the group.

"Council is in emergency session. No admittance."

"We are Methuselahs. We don't recognize your authority."

"Recognize this." One of the guards drew a side arm and thrust it into Joe's face. "Beat it."

Lizzy was forced to one side as the guard leveled his gun at Joe. It was a simple matter for her to extract a blade and lay it against the guard's throat. The other knife touched his leg near the femoral artery. He stiffened.

"Is this worth dying for?" She pricked the knife into the guard's leg. "Think quickly." The big man opened his hand and let Joe take his gun. Roberta had her cane up against the other guard.

"Walk away now," Joe said softly. "Don't look back, don't come back, and I will forget this ever happened. He tossed Grant's cane on the floor in front of them. "You might want to check on your boss to see what happens to traitors."

The pair fled down the carpeted hall. Joe watched them reach the door to the stairs and go through.

"Lock the entrance to the top floor, Devon," Joe spoke into his phone. "No one gets in until we're done here."

He put the gun in his pocket and pushed the doors open.

Evil has a face

The empty Council Chamber was furnished in dark oaks and thick carpet. Rich paintings in gold frames adorned the walls.

"This way." Roberta walked to an inconspicuous opening beside a heavy tapestry. It opened at her touch and they walked through.

The Council met in a room painted hospital green. Medical equipment hissed and beeped. Old men and women sat in special chairs around the table. At the end sat a monitor with Councilor Molloy's face. Another monitor with a Councilor's face sat midway. Red wrinkled her nose at the smell in the room.

"It's the stench of fear." Joe walked to where he could be seen by everyone. "Fear is an appalling motivation for making decisions."

"You have no right to be here, Methuselah," one of the men said. "Even your powers stop at that door."

"Not tonight." He walked over to the speaker. "There is treason in the air tonight."

"Yes," one of the women said. "People need to go back to work. If we must we will compel them."

"Is it treason to want to have a good life?" Trey asked. "Is it treason to keep your earnings instead of having them confiscated? Is it treason to reject being valued as only a repository for organs?"

"You are young. You don't understand the implications."

"I am not young, and I ask the same questions," Joe said.

"Ruling a country is complicated, Methuselah," Councilor Molloy's image spoke with a machine twang.

"So complicated you need to live a hundred, two hundred, three hundred years to understand it?"

"If that's what it takes."

"And if you need to destroy the country to achieve immortality?"

"I am the Chair of the Council of the Eldest. I have the right."

"You have the right to destroy the country?" one of the women asked. The other members of the Council muttered. Joe indicated a computer in the corner and wiggled his fingers at Red. She nodded, slipped over and started tapping keys.

"You're weak. You will die. You don't matter." Molloy's face on the monitor twisted in contempt. "You're *old.* All of you. Only I am strong. Only I will live forever. Tonight, I reshape the country."

Red waved at Joe and pointed to an exit. He nodded. She shifted over to Trey and whispered a few words. He rose and Lizzy followed them out of the room.

"Roberta has some evidence and some questions for you. You *will* answer them. There will be changes, and it starts with this. None of you is immune from Justice."

"You can't touch us, Methuselah," an old man said. "We are beyond your directives. We'll deal with Molloy and then continue with our agenda."

Joe strode to a wall and jerked on a plug. A machine stopped hissing as it ceased to breathe for the Councilor. The old man's eyes went wide, then blank. Alarms rang, and white-coated medics rushed into the room. Joe watched them work on the decrepit old man. Finally they lifted him onto a gurney and prepared to wheel him out to the emergency elevator.

"Take him to a hospice. Make sure he gets proper care."

"He is a Councilor!"

"Not anymore," Joe replied. "He betrayed his oath. He served himself before his country." They rolled the gurney out. It was obvious the paramedics didn't view their charge with quite the same reverence.

"Are you going to pull all their plugs?" the man in the second monitor sneered. "You can't reach mine."

"If I must." Joe walked around the room to look each councilor in the eye. "I wonder how many medics are on duty tonight. With all the chaos, some of them may have left." He wandered toward another machine. "Security seems to have failed too." He sauntered over to the monitor. "My people know where you are Councilor."

"Don't, please," begged the old woman who was hooked to the machine he approached. "Tell us your charges."

"You have allowed your fear of death to destroy the lives of millions. You have allowed monsters to sit in your midst without protest."

Roberta went to the computer in the corner and inserted a thumb drive. Images began streaming across the screen on the wall behind her.

"These are pictures of children being bought and sold," she said. "These are pictures of children who have been abused, then murdered."

"We have police forces to deal with those crimes," said a Councilor.

"Not if this office protects the criminals from investigation. That makes it my business. It makes it your business."

"Why should we care about a few children?"

"Because it's your job to care. If you don't care, it is time for you to leave." Roberta waved her cane in the old man's face. "What benefit are you, if you degrade the people you are working for?"

"We don't work for them. We rule. They work for us." Molloy's image suddenly flashed to the side, then the screen went blank.

"I think it is time to find a new Council. We will ensure you are well supported." Joe tugged on the computer plug then disconnected the cords to the still-functioning monitor.

"Roberta will guard you until you are moved to

a hospice."

***

In the passageway, Red spoke briefly.

"I have a trace on Molloy's location. He is here in this building, a few floors down. I think it is time we had a talk with him."

Lizzy flexed her fingers a few times and muttered to herself. Trey nodded. The trio jogged to the stairs. Doors clicked, then swung open. Lizzy insisted on leading in case the guards were still lurking nearby. But the stairs were clear. The flashlights shone bright circles on the steps and left the rest in darkness. Trey descended warily, but they reached Molloy's floor without incident.

This hallway was carpeted, but not as lavishly as the one leading to the Council Chambers. Through the obscurity, they followed the ovals of the flashlights to the only door with light leaking from underneath.

"He must be hooked up to the same generator as the Council. They can't risk losing the power to their life support."

"Or he has his own. I don't see him trusting someone else."

"The door is locked. This is where we need Jimmy."

"Let me see if I can remember anything Jimmy taught me." Trey extracted the picks from his shoe. "I got used to carrying them. Now, it depends on whether the emergency power is connected to the lock." He fiddled with the catch. *I should have practiced more.* The pick slid in a millimeter. No jolt. A few minutes later, the door clicked and swung open.

A bare bulb hung from the ceiling, lighting the hollow front room. No furniture remained. Faded spaces on the walls marked where paintings had been removed. Wires dangled from switch boxes in the walls. Trey shrugged and pointed to a doorway with a glow emanating from beneath it.

They listened. Hearing no sound, Red took a deep breath and with a toe, pushed the door. The room had been painted a stark white over wallpaper, which had started to peel. The floor was splattered with paint, and the carpet rolled up against a wall. A hospital bed sat against another wall. The bed was obscured by a myriad of wires and tubes snaking from it to a bank of machines. Some monitored heart rate and blood pressure, others showed strange jagged lines scrawling across the screens. One of the screens showed the Council Chamber. Roberta was gesturing with her cane at a sullen Councilor.

Councilor Molloy walked into the room. His face flushed bright red. He hit a key on the computer and it went blank.

He looked at Lizzy. "You and I have a conversation to finish." He lifted a baton from his belt. "I am prepared this time." He lunged at Lizzy. The baton clanged on the bed's metal rail. Sparks flew. Lizzy eyed the baton then sheathed her knives.

"Be careful, you fool." Another Councilor Molloy walked into the room from a door on the other side of the bed. "He's such a klutz. He just had to have the stupid stick, but it will keep him out of trouble while we talk."

An arm snaked around Trey's neck, and he instinctively lurched away. A third Molloy strode towards Trey, grunting malevolently.

"He isn't much of a conversationalist. But he does know what he wants." The second Molloy walked toward Red and casually backhanded her. She managed to block most of the force with her arm, but Trey could see the blow had struck home. She cradled her arm and backed away. The man moved in again, and she did a snap kick to his knee, which should have sent him to the floor in agony. He paused a second, then threw another punch she narrowly avoided.

"A pity the replicas can't hold on to their humanity. Some fault in the way the mind is loaded into the body. We last a month, perhaps two, then we get fixated on certain parts of our personality. We have memories, but they become less and less a guide to our actions. We tend to want things more...visceral. That's where you come in, boy. You hold the secret of a viable clone in your genes, and we intend to have it."

The room was large, but with the bed, equipment, three young people and the three Molloys it was crowded. The Molloys didn't seem to care who they struck, as long as they were wounding. Trey was almost swiped by the baton's back swing. His hair stood up in response to the stick's electric charge. The lumbering Molloy tripped up Red and was trying to land a kick. Trey kicked the back of the Molloy's leg and he collapsed.

"I'm not a clone, you moron." Trey helped Red to her feet while pulling her out of range of the Molloy Number Three, who was still talking.

"Oh, you are a clone, why else would your father have created you? You are the means to his immortality." The talkative copy leaned against the wall.

Red continued to cradle her arm, and now limping, she sidestepped the lumbering Molloy who'd attacked her again.

Lizzy screamed as the baton brushed her leg. She dropped to the floor, her leg twitching uncontrollably. The Molloy with the baton smiled cruelly and prepared to shock her again. She reached for her knives but couldn't control her hands.

"No!" Red shouted, but the talking Molloy succeeded in blocking her from coming to Lizzy's aid.

The arm came around Trey's throat again as the lumbering copy attacked after bouncing off the partition. Instead of recoiling, Trey grasped the arm and lunged forward carrying the grunting Molloy on his back. Trey landed on top of Lizzy with the Molloy on his back just as the baton came down. The electricity shot through his body, setting his limbs moving in a spastic dance. The Molloy screamed and flung himself away. He landed between Trey and the baton wielder. A brief moment of confusion crossed the Molloy's face before it twitched and went still.

Trey dragged himself to his feet and felt Lizzy pass him a knife. He straddled Lizzy and eyed the

Molloy in front of him.

"My father wanted a son to love, not to become a monster."

Red gasped behind him, she was in trouble. He swiveled and saw the last Molloy, finally silent, his hands around Red's neck. She was punching his face, with no effect. Trey hurled the knife at the Molloy, but it hit flat and dropped to the floor.

"Watch out," Lizzy rasped a warning from below him.

Trey stepped backward inside the blow. He grabbed the baton-wielding Molloy's arm and pivoted adding momentum to the blow, then twisted away. The Molloy staggered back and Trey's kick registered square in the chest. It was just enough to send him back against the bed. He tried to catch himself, but the baton touched the bed rail. The arc of electricity blinded Trey for a second, and he staggered back, tripping over Lizzy. The Molloy fell twitching the floor.

Trey rolled over and tried to stand so he could help Red but his legs refused to work. Lizzy tossed a knife. Red grabbed it and slammed it into the Molloy's temple then fell to the floor gasping for air. He stood and wrenched the knife out.

"Won't help you this time." The talkative Molloy switched the grip on the knife and knelt beside her. "I haven't cut anyone's throat for a while." Trey watched helplessly as the Molloy lowered the knife. Red tried to move, but the Molloy kneeled on her chest. "You can't kill me. I am going to live forever."

The first shot struck him between the eyes. The

Molloy collapsed backward. The next shot bored a hole in the hand holding the knife, sending the blade skittering across the floor. Joe put the next two shots through the wires and tubes into the faint lump under the sheets. He emptied the rest of the shells into the bank of computers. With all the wires disconnected he stomped on the computers until pieces were scattered around the room.

"Nobody lives forever," Joe said. "Devon got worried about you. Sorry it took a while to find you."

Trey dragged himself over to Red.

"Are you alright?" he asked.

"Now there is a truly brilliant question," Red rasped. "Just kiss me." So he did. When he finished he kissed her again.

"Are you crying?" she said.

"I thought I was going to lose you," he said.

"You won't get rid of me that easy."

Trey looked around at the ravaged room. Joe knelt beside Lizzy, holding her hand.

"I don't think it was easy." Trey kissed Red again. "I want to stay with you the rest of my life."

She gazed into his eyes. He could lose himself in those depths.

"What's the magic word?" she whispered.

"I love you," Trey whispered back, aches and pains vanishing along with the world around him.

"That'll do." She pulled him into another kiss. "I love you too."

Trey eased Red into a sitting position and they leaned against the wall. Joe maneuvered Lizzy to a place beside them.

"You better treat her right." Lizzy kissed Trey on the forehead. "I'll be watching you."

Joe looked at the three of them, and shook his head. He lowered himself beside Lizzy.

"This was the easy part," he said. "The hard part will be setting the country to rights. I hope you don't think I am going to do it by myself."

"My dad will help," Red said.

"And mine, when he gets home from Japan."

"I need *you*. You wanted a world where young people are valued. You are going to help create it."

"Sure thing." Trey leaned his head against Red's. "We'll start tomorrow."

NEW TRICKS FOR AN OLD DOG

Putting the country back together was both simpler and more complicated than Joe had expected. The news of Molloy's plot had rocked the nation, and rapid changes were made to prevent a recurrence. But old habits die hard, and before long some of the elderly began to resent the incursion of younger and more boisterous people into their neighborhoods. Constant bickering between the generations was going to take more than legislation to change. The Youth Reserves were a special sticking point. Oddly, it was the youth in the Reserves who didn't want them to be closed. They wanted their education before being tossed out into the world.

Joe ensured youth sedation ceased immediately. It solved some problems and caused some new ones. The youth were more boisterous, but they were also more prepared to learn. Joe put Harry Destnir in charge of retooling the curriculum.

"Joe," Harry had said, "I hope you don't expect me to thank you."

"No," Joe said, "but I do expect you to do an effective job."

Harry had laughed and hung up, but within a week there was a draft for "A New Instructional Paradigm" on the Councilor for Education's desk.

"I wonder what Mr. Destnir would think if he knew I was examining his work?" Trey chuckled.

"From what you've said about him, he'd probably be pleased." Red laughed, looking over his shoulder at the proposal. "So of all the jobs Joe offered you, why take the assistant to the Councilor for Education?"

"Because it's the most important job."

"That's my man." Red smiled and hugged him.

The Chief met them at the Elder Justice building for the new Council Chair's first address to the nation. It was going to take Trey a while to adjust to saying Councilor Jones instead of Chief. Jones was the second appointee to the Council. His first motion was to restore democratic elections and allow every contributing member of society to vote. Discussions about the definition were long and heated. Two members of the Council found it overwhelming and resigned. The new Chair of the Council breathed deeply and let the discussion continue. In the meantime Joe arranged for the restoration of power and encouraged the people to return to work.

"This is a time for change," he said on the vid. "We need to learn to listen to each other once more. We must value every member of our society equally, young and old, rich and poor. It means giving up assumptions we have held dear for close to a century. We can no longer look at a person and think we know them. If we are going to move forward, we have to do better."

"I hate talking on the vid," Joe said.

"Think of it as atoning," his new assistant said.

"Lizzy." Joe laughed. "I think you're right." He poured her a coffee. "Are you coming to the club tonight?"

"I wouldn't miss it," she said. "Though I'll have to get busy. The Council Chair's office is a lot busier than a Methuselah's. I don't see why you didn't keep Devon on."

"I wanted her to support Roberta with her investigations. If Devon is out there, I know she'll keep me honest."

"Hey." Red stuck her head around the corner. "Are you ready to go? Trey's waiting."

"On our way, dear." Joe got up. He'd abandoned the cane since creating a requirement for all Councilors to be prepared to appear in public without life support. Lizzy still carried her knives. He was as safe as he wanted to be.

They walked out, and found Red and Trey holding hands while they waited. He smiled at them and led the way to the car.

***

The club was just the way he remembered it. Once again, the music flowed like good whisky across his ears. Once again, retirees packed the tables. Joe and his friends sat at the same table as he had before. The waitress came to take their orders. She struggled, and managed to smile at Red, Trey and

Lizzy, but it was Maggie who brought their orders. She sat down with them. The law would change much faster than prejudices.

"So you did it. You changed the world. What are you going to do tomorrow?"

"Change it again." Joe sipped from his whisky.

"Keep changing it until we get it right." Trey swirled the ice in his glass.

"Have some fun too." Red took Trey's hand.

"To tomorrow!" Trey lifted his glass in a toast. Red clinked her glass against his.

"The future is for the young." Joe said as he lifted his glass. "I will stick with today. It's all we ever have."

"Today is good," Lizzy said.

"Today is great." Red kissed Trey. He just smiled and nodded.

Joe looked at Trey and Red. They had their arms around each other and her head was on his shoulder. *Those two are enough to make me believe in a better world.*

The saxophone player started a new song, and winked him. All wasn't right in the world, yet. But they were closer today then yesterday, and maybe, if they worked diligently, tomorrow would be better still.

ACKNOWLEDGEMENTS

Any book is a team effort. The author scribbles ideas and if they're lucky and work hard, come up with a workable story. Then the hard work comes in, with editors like Dean C. Moore, critique circles and beta readers. I have to thank the good people at CritiqueCircle.com who read and commented on a barely polished draft.

Then Kai Wong, Deborah Dunson and Rachael Eliker who beta read for me and gave invaluable advice on the story.

And Esther Fyk who copy-edited and proofread for me, pointing out all the sentences which really didn't make any sense, or paragraph in which all the sentences started with the same word.

Finally, as always, my wife and muse, Alexandra who forces me to read my books out loud to her and puts up with long periods when I'm vanished into my office.

About the Author

Alex is an author, editor and reviewer living in Winnipeg, Manitoba overlooking the Assiniboine River. He has two dogs who drag him out for walks, a wife who makes him read out loud and a scotch collection to celebrate the successful completion of his next goal.

Other Works by Alex

The Regent's Reign
Calliope and the Sea Serpent
Wendigo Whispers
The Gods Above
The Heronmaster
Blood and Sparkles and other stories
Princess of Boring
By the Book
Sarcasm is My Superpower
Tales of Light and Dark
Like Mushrooms (poetry and photography)
Playing on Yggdrasil
The Unenchanted Princess

Alex also has stories in:

Canadian Creatures
Song of the Axe
Words on the Rocks
Beyond the Wail
Collidor Stream Collection 2016